EX LIBRIS

VINTAGE CLASSICS

SIMONE DE BEAUVOIR

Simone de Beauvoir was born in Paris in 1908. In 1929 she became the youngest person ever to obtain the *agrégation* in philosophy at the Sorbonne, placing second to Jean-Paul Sartre. She taught at the lycées at Marseille and Rouen from 1931–1937, and in Paris from 1938–1943. After the war she emerged as one of the leaders of the existentialist movement, working with Sartre on *Les Temps modernes*. The author of several books including *The Mandarins* (1954), which was awarded the Prix Goncourt, de Beauvoir was one of the most influential thinkers of her generation. She died in 1986.

LAUREN ELKIN

Lauren Elkin is the author of several books, including *Scaffolding*, *Art Monsters* and *Flâneuse*, as well as the translator of Simone de Beauvoir's previously unpublished novel *The Inseparables*. After twenty years in Paris, she now lives in London.

SIMONE DE BEAUVOIR

THE IMAGE OF HER

TRANSLATED FROM THE FRENCH BY
Lauren Elkin

VINTAGE CLASSICS

1 3 5 7 9 10 8 6 4 2

Vintage Classics is part of the Penguin Random House
group of companies whose addresses can be found
at global.penguinrandomhouse.com

Penguin
Random House
UK

This translation first published in Great Britain with the title *The Image of Her* in 2025
First published in France with the title *Les Belles Images* by Éditions Gallimard in 1966

This translation has been supported by an Authors'
Foundation grant from the Society of Authors

penguin.co.uk/vintage-classics

Typeset in 12/14.75pt Bembo Book MT Pro by Jouve (UK), Milton Keynes
Printed and bound in Great Britain by Clays Ltd, Elcograf S.p.A.

The authorised representative in the EEA is Penguin Random House Ireland,
Morrison Chambers, 32 Nassau Street, Dublin D02 YH68

A CIP catalogue record for this book is available from the British Library

ISBN 9781784879907

To Claude Lanzmann

1

— What an extraordinary October, said Gisèle Dufrène.

They all agree, they smile, the summer heat falls from the grey-blue sky – what do they have that I don't? – their gazes skim the scene before them, straight out of *Plaisir de France* or *Votre Maison*, the farm bought for next to nothing, all right, a little more than that, and done up by Jean-Charles at great expense (*Give or take a million*, said Gilbert), the roses against the stone wall, the chrysanthemums, the asters, the dahlias, *the most beautiful in the whole Ile-de-France*, said Dominique, the screen and the blue and violet chairs – how daring! – breaking up the green of the lawn, ice clinking in the glasses. Houdan kisses Dominique's hand. She is slim in her black trousers and bright shirt, her hair very light, somewhere between blonde and white; from behind she looks no older than thirty. *Nobody knows how to entertain like you, Dominique.* (At exactly this moment, in another garden, completely different, but exactly the same, someone is pronouncing these same words and the same smile appears on someone else's face. *What a magnificent Sunday!* Why am I thinking this?)

Everything was perfect: the sun and the breeze, the barbecue, the thick steaks, the salads, the fruit, the wine. Gilbert told stories of his hunting trips in Kenya, and then he became absorbed by this Japanese puzzle – he had six more pieces to put in their places – and Laurence suggested they play the Ferryman's Challenge, that sounds like fun, they love to astonish themselves and laugh at each other.[1] It takes a lot out of her, that's why she feels depressed now, I go in cycles. Louise is playing with her cousins in the rear of the garden; Catherine is reading before the fireplace where a feeble flame goes on burning; she looks like all those happy young girls who like to read, lying stretched out on the carpet. *Don Quixote*. Last week it was *Quentin Durward*, but that's not why she was crying in the night. Why then? Louise was very upset about it. *Maman, Catherine is sad, she cries at night*. She likes her teachers, she has a new best friend, she looks well, the house is a happy one.

— Still trying to come up with a slogan? says Dufrène.

— Somehow I have to convince people to cover their walls with wood panelling.

When she daydreams, people think she's trying to come up with an advertising slogan. It's useful. Around her everyone is talking about Jeanne Texcier's failed suicide attempt. A cigarette in her left hand, her right hand open and raised as if to ward off interruptions, Dominique says, in her throaty, authoritarian voice:

— She's not very bright, if she has a career it's thanks to her husband, but in any case, when you're one of the most high-profile women in Paris, you don't behave like a simpering little shop girl!

In another garden, completely different, but exactly the same, someone is saying: *Dominique Langlois? If she has a career it's thanks to Gilbert Mortier*. And it's not fair, she got into the radio business by the back door in '45, and she fought her way to get where she is, she worked like a dog, trampling right over anyone who got in her way. Why did they take such pleasure in tearing each other to pieces? They also say, and Gisèle Dufrène thinks it for sure, that if Maman got her hooks into Gilbert it was out of self-interest. It's true she could never have afforded this house or these trips without him, but he brought her something else, too; she was completely distraught after she left Papa (he moped around the house like a lost soul, how callously she left him as soon as Marthe was married); it's thanks to Gilbert that she became such a strong, confident woman. (Of course, there were less charitable ways of looking at it.)

Hubert and Marthe return from the forest with their arms full of foliage. Head back, a smile frozen on her lips, briskly she marches on, like a saint drunk on God's happy love. That was the role she had played since she'd found religion. They return to their places on the blue and violet cushions, Hubert lights the pipe that he is doubtless the last man in France to call *my old puffer*. His frozen smile, his excessive padding. When he travels he wears black sunglasses, saying *I love to travel incognito*. A very good dentist who conscientiously keeps up with the horse races in his spare time. I understand why Marthe had to invent her own sources of satisfaction.

— In Europe, in the summer, there's not an inch of room to lie down on any of the beaches, says Dominique. In Bermuda, there are immense beaches, nearly deserted, where nobody knows you.

— For travellers on a budget, says Laurence, deadpan.

— And Tahiti? Why didn't you go back to Tahiti, Gisèle asks.

— In 1955, Tahiti was great. But now it's worse than Saint-Tropez. So banal.

Twenty years ago. Papa suggested Florence, or Grenada, and she'd said *Everyone goes there, it's so banal*. The four of them tooling around in the car like the Fenouillard family, she'd joked. He went walking without us in Italy and Greece, and we holidayed in chic places; at least, Dominique thought they were chic at the time. Now she crosses the ocean to sunbathe. For Christmas, Gilbert is taking her to Baalbek.

— They say they have magnificent beaches in Brazil, totally empty, says Gisèle. And you can stop off in Brasília. I would so like to see Brasília!

— Oh, no! says Laurence. The housing estates around Paris are depressing enough. But a whole city of them?

— You're just like your father, says Dominique. So old-fashioned.

— Who isn't? asks Jean-Charles. Even nowadays, when they're inventing rockets and robots, people still think as though it's the nineteenth century.

— Not me, says Dominique.

— But you, you are exceptional in every way, says Gilbert in a conclusive tone (or an emphatic one, rather; he always keeps an ironic distance from whatever it is he's saying).

— At any rate, the construction workers who built the city share my opinion: they chose to keep their wooden houses.

— They hardly had a choice in the matter, dear Laurence, says Gilbert. The rent in Brasília is more than they can afford. The hint of a smile slightly curved his mouth, as if he were apologising for his superiority.

— Brasília is over, says Dufrène. It's stuck in the kind of architectural vision where the roof, a door, the wall, and the fireplace each have their own distinct existence. What we're trying to do now is create a synthesised house, where each element is versatile – the roof blends into the wall and flows into the middle of the courtyard.

Laurence is unhappy with herself; she has said something

idiotic, clearly. Look at what comes of talking about things you don't understand. *Never talk about things you don't understand*, Mlle Houchet used to say. But in that case one would never open one's mouth to speak. She silently listens to Jean-Charles describe the city of the future. For no discernible reason, it delights him, the idea of these wonders to come, which he will never see with his own eyes. He was so pleased to learn that today's man is several centimetres taller than medieval man, who himself was taller than prehistoric man. They're lucky to be able to get so interested in things. Once again, just as heatedly, Dufrène and Jean-Charles are debating the crisis in architecture.

— They have to find the funding, of course, says Jean-Charles, but by other means. To give up on the power of dissuasion would be to fall out of History.

Nobody answers; in the silence comes Marthe's ecstatic voice:

— If only people would collectively agree on disarmament! Have you read Pope Paul VI's latest message?

Dominique cuts her off with impatience.

— People who have every right to think so have told me that if war broke out, it would take just twenty years for humanity to return to our present level of civilisation.

Gilbert raises his head, he has only four pieces left to place.

— There won't be a war. The gap between capitalist countries and socialist ones will soon disappear entirely.

Because just now we're in the midst of the great revolution of the twentieth century: producing is more important than possessing.

So why spend so much money arming ourselves? Laurence wonders. But Gilbert has an answer for everything, and she's not about to put her foot in it again. In any case, Jean-Charles has already replied: *Without the bomb, we would fall out of History*. What does that mean, exactly? It would surely be a catastrophe, everyone looks very worried.

Gilbert turns amiably towards her.

— You must come on Friday. I want to play you my new high-fidelity system.

— The same one as Karim and Alexander of Yugoslavia, says Dominique.

— It's truly a marvel. Once you've heard it, you can never go back to listening to music on an ordinary machine.

— Then I really don't want to hear it, says Laurence. I so love listening to music. (It's not true, actually. I'm just saying that to be funny.)

Jean-Charles seems very interested:

— How much do you have to pay, minimum, to get a really good high-fidelity stereo?

— At the least, the very least, you can get a mono speaker for 300,000 old francs. But this isn't that, not at all.

— To have something really good, do you think you have to spend around a million? asks Dufrène.

— Listen: a good speaker, in mono, is worth at least

600,000 to a million. In stereo, at least two million. I recommend getting mono rather than a mediocre stereo. A good amp-preamp will run you about 500,000 francs.

— That's what I said, at least a million, says Dufrène with a sigh.

— There are worse ways to spend a million francs, says Gilbert.

— If Vergne gets the Roussillon job, I'm buying us one, says Jean-Charles to Laurence. He turns to Dominique:

— He has this incredible idea for one of those vacation complexes they're building there.

— Vergne always has incredible ideas. But they do not often see the light of day, says Dufrène.

— They will. Do you know him? Jean-Charles asks Gilbert. He's amazing to work with; the whole studio is so enthusiastic. They're not just carrying out plans, they're creating something.

— He's the greatest architect of his generation, Dominique says. At the very avant-garde of urban planning.

— Still, I would rather be on Monnod's team, says Dufrène. We're not creating something, we're just carrying out plans. But we make more money.

Hubert takes his pipe from his mouth.

— He's got a point.

Laurence gets up; she smiles at her mother:

— Can I steal a few of your dahlias?

— Of course.

Marthe gets up as well; she steers her sister off to the side.

— Did you see Papa on Wednesday? How is he?

— At the house he's always in a good mood. He fought with Jean-Charles, for a change.

— Jean-Charles doesn't understand Papa either.

Marthe gazes up at the heavens.

— He's so different from other people. There's something other-worldly about him. Music, poetry – for him they're a form of prayer.

Laurence leans over the dahlias; this kind of language annoys her. Of course he has something about him that the others don't, that I don't (but what else do they have that I also lack?). Roses, red, yellow, almost orange. She holds the magnificent dahlias tightly in her hand.

— Did you have a good day, my darlings? asks Dominique.

— Marvellous, says Marthe fervently.

— Marvellous, Laurence echoes.

The light is fading, she's not upset about having to leave. She hesitates. She's waited until the last minute; asking her mother for something still intimidates her as much now as it did when she was fifteen.

— There's something I want to ask you.

— What is it? Dominique's voice is cold.

— About Serge. He wants to leave university. He'd like to work in radio or television.

— Did your father put you up to this?

— I met Bernard and Georgette at Papa's.

— How are they? Are they still playing at Baucis and Philemon?

— Oh, I barely saw them.

— Tell your father once and for all that I am not an employment agency. I think it's disgraceful the way people try to take advantage of me. I've never asked anything of anyone.

— You can't blame Papa for wanting to help his nephew, says Marthe.

— I blame him for not being able to do anything himself. Dominique held up a hand to ward off protest. If he was a man of religion, if he'd joined the Trappists, I could understand. (Oh no, thinks Laurence.) But he chose mediocrity instead.

She could not forgive him for having become a parliamentary draftsman and not the brilliant lawyer she thought she was marrying. A dead end, she called him.

— It's late, says Laurence. I'm going to go and powder my nose.

She could not stand by and let her mother attack her father, but to defend him would be worse. Always this pang in the heart when she thought of him, this feeling of regret. For no reason: I've never taken Maman's side.

— I'm going up as well, I have to change, says Dominique.

— I'll look after the children, says Marthe.

Convenient. Ever since she'd entered the sainthood, she appropriated all drudgery to herself. Her joys are so lofty that we can leave her to them without feeling guilty about it.

Touching up her hair in her mother's bedroom – this Spanish rustic decor really is too pretty – Laurence makes one last attempt:

— Is there really nothing you can do for Serge?

— No.

Dominique joins her at the mirror.

— Would you look at the state of me! At my age, a woman who works all day and goes out every night ends up looking a wreck. I've got to get some sleep.

Laurence scrutinises her mother in the mirror. She is perfect, the very picture of a woman who is ageing well. *A woman who is ageing.* Dominique refuses this image of herself. She is showing weakness for the first time. Illness, hard knocks, until now she's taken it all in her stride. But suddenly she looks panicked:

— I can't believe I'll be seventy one day.

— You're holding up better than any other woman, says Laurence.

— My body, fine, there's no one I envy. But look at this.

She indicates around her eyes, her neck. It's clear she's no longer in her forties.

— OK, you're no longer in your twenties, says Laurence. But loads of men prefer women who've lived a bit. Look at Gilbert.

— Gilbert, she says. I'm killing myself going out like this, all to keep him. It may come back to haunt me.

— Let's go then!

Dominique puts on her Balenciaga suit. Never Chanel, people spend a fortune on it just to look like they got dressed at a flea market. She mutters:

— That bitch Marie-Claire. She obstinately refuses to divorce him, just to annoy me.

— She'll give in eventually.

Marie-Claire is surely saying: *that bitch Dominique*. Back in the days of Lucile de Saint-Chamont, Gilbert still lived with his wife, no questions asked. Lucile had a husband and children. Dominique had forced him to separate from Marie-Claire; if he had given in it was because it suited him, of course, but all the same, Laurence had thought her mother had acted somewhat aggressively.

— Look, living with Gilbert isn't without risks. He loves his freedom.

— As do you.

— Yes.

Dominique turns this way and that in front of the three-panel mirror and smiles. In fact, she is delighted to dine with the Verdelets; she is genuinely impressed by government ministers. How malicious I am, thinks Laurence. She's her mother; she feels affection towards her. But she is also a stranger. Who is hiding behind the images that dance across the mirrors? Maybe no one at all.

— Is all well with you?

— Yes, fine. I go from triumph to triumph.

— The girls?

— You've seen them. They're thriving.

Dominique asks questions as a matter of good form, but she would find it indiscreet if Laurence's answers were in any way worrying, or even detailed.

In the garden, Jean-Charles leans on the back of Gisèle's chair, a subtle form of flirtation which flatters them both (and Dufrène as well, if you ask me), they give the impression that they could have the affair that neither of them actually wants. (And what if they did? I don't think I would mind. Can there be love without jealousy?)

— All right, I'm counting on you for Friday, says Gilbert. It's no fun when you're not there.

— Oh, come on!

— I promise you.

He shakes Laurence's hand as if they shared a special mutual understanding; that's why everyone thinks he's so charming.

— Till Friday.

People are always insisting she come over, they love coming to see her, she really doesn't understand why.

— What a marvellous day, says Gisèle.

— With life in Paris what it is, we really need to relax like this, says Jean-Charles.

— Absolutely indispensable, says Gilbert.

Laurence helps the girls into the back seat of the car, doors locked. She sits beside Jean-Charles, and they drive up the narrow road behind Dufrène's DS.

— What's amazing about Gilbert is that he has remained so humble, says Jean-Charles. Think about all the responsibilities he has, his power. And not the slightest trace of self-importance.

— He can afford humility.

— You don't like him. It's normal. But don't be unfair.

— But of course I like him. (Does she really like him? She likes everyone.) Gilbert doesn't go on about it, you're right, she says. But no one is left unaware that he directs two of the largest electronic machine corporations in the world, or the role he's playing in the creation of a common market.

— I wonder how much money he makes. It must be practically limitless.

— It would terrify me to have so much money.

— He uses it wisely.

— Yes.

It's strange: when he's telling those stories about his travels, Gilbert is hilarious. But an hour later, it's hard to remember what he said.

— A truly successful weekend! says Jean-Charles.

— Yes, a real success.

And again, Laurence asks herself: what do they have that I don't? Oh, I shouldn't worry this way, there are days like this when I get out of bed on the wrong side, and can find no pleasure in anything! She should be used to it. Yet every time she wonders. Something's not right; what is it? And she suddenly feels indifferent, distant, as if she belonged somewhere else. When she had been depressed five years ago they had explained it to her: many young women experience this kind of crisis; Dominique had encouraged her to get out of the house, to work, and Jean-Charles was very enthusiastic about it when he saw how much money I made. Now there's no longer any reason to fall apart. There's work ahead of me, people all around me, I'm happy with my life. No, no danger. It's just a mood. I'm sure it happens to other people and they don't make a whole drama out of it. She turns to the children:

— Did you have a good time, my darlings?

— Oh, yes! says Louise, energetically.

The smell of dead leaves comes in through the open window; the stars shine in the sky in a way that reminds her of childhood and Laurence suddenly feels completely well.

The Ferrari shoots past them, Dominique waves her hand, her light scarf floats in the wind, she is really very attractive. And Gilbert looks very well for fifty-six. A real couple. She was right, on the whole, to demand an unambiguous role in his life.

— They're well met, says Jean-Charles. They're an attractive couple for their age.

A couple. Laurence studies Jean-Charles. She likes sitting beside him while he drives. He keeps his eyes on the road and she looks at his profile, which so moved her ten years ago, which she still finds very touching. Looked at face on, he isn't quite the same – she no longer sees him the same way. He has an intelligent, lively face, but also – how to put it – frozen, like all other faces. Looked at in profile, in the dusky half-light, his mouth seems less decided, his eyes more dreamy. That is how he appeared to her eleven years earlier, and how she imagines him when he is not there, and then sometimes again in fleeting moments like this one, riding beside him in the car. They don't speak. There is a complicity to their silence, expressive of an understanding too profound for words. An illusion perhaps. But for as long as the road rushes along beneath their wheels, as the children doze, as Jean-Charles is quiet, Laurence wants to believe in it.

A little while later, all her anxiety fades away when Laurence sits down at her table. She is just a bit tired, dazed from all that fresh air, the kind of state in which her mind begins to wander, which Dominique used to interrupt briskly: *Don't just sit and daydream, do something*. The kind of mood that lately she had forbidden herself from indulging in. *I have to come up with an idea*, she says to herself, unscrewing the cap from her pen. What a pretty picture all this must make, promising – to the benefit of some furniture designer, or shirtmaker, or florist – security, happiness. A couple, walking below, along the parapet as the trees whisper overhead, will be able to look in on this idealised interior: lamplight; a young, elegant man in an angora wool jumper attentively reading a magazine, and a young woman sitting at her desk, a pen in her hand, the harmony of blacks, reds and yellows nicely complementing (oh, happy chance) the red and yellow dahlias. Earlier, when I cut them, they were living flowers. Laurence thinks of the king who turned all he touched to gold, even his daughter, who became a resplendent metal doll. Everything she touches turns into an image. *Wood panelling: where urban chic meets the poetry of the forest.* Through the leaves she glimpses the water, blackly lapping; a boat passes by, searching the banks with its white gaze. Its light splashes on the windows, brutally illuminating the lovers walking arm in arm, a flash of the past for me, just as I am now the tender image of their future, with the children they might guess are asleep in the bedrooms at the back of the flat. *Children will feel as though they've climbed into a hollow tree, in their delightful bedroom with natural wood panelling.* An idea worth considering.

She has always been a picture. Dominique made sure of it, Dominique who in her own childhood had been transfixed by pictures of lives that differed so radically from her own, completely determined, drawing on all her intelligence and substantial energy, to fill the inner void. (You don't know what it is to have torn slippers and to feel through your sock that you have stepped in a gob of spit. You don't know what it is to be judged by girls with clean hair, who look at you and nudge each other. No, you will not leave the house with that stain on your skirt, go and change immediately.) An impeccable little girl, a hard-working teenager, a perfect young woman. You were so clean, so fresh, so perfect, says Jean-Charles.

Everything was clean, fresh, perfect: the blue water of the swimming pool, the luxurious sound made by the tennis balls, the white mountains, like stone needles, the rounded clouds in the smooth sky, the scent of pine. Every morning, as she opened her shutters, Laurence saw something from a sublime, glossy photograph. On the hotel grounds, the boys and girls in light-coloured clothing, skin healthy and tanned, burnished by the sun like beautiful stones. And Laurence and Jean-Charles dressed in light colours, tanned, burnished. Suddenly one evening, coming back from a drive, in the parked car, his mouth on my own, this blazing disruption, this vertigo. And so, for days and weeks, I was no longer a picture, but flesh and blood, desire, pleasure. And I rediscovered that secret joy that I used to know, sitting at my father's feet or holding his hand in mine. And again, eighteen months ago, with Lucien – fire in my veins, my bones exquisitely liquefying. She bites her lip. If Jean-Charles knew! In reality nothing has changed between them. Lucien is marginal. And in any case she no longer feels for him the way she did before.

— How's that idea coming along?

— Getting closer.

The husband's attentive look; the young wife's pretty smile. She's often been told that her smile is pretty; she feels it on her lips. The idea will come; it's always hard in the beginning, so many used-up, clichéd turns of phrase, traps to avoid. But she's good at what she does. I'm not selling wood panelling; I'm selling security, success, and a touch of poetry. When Dominique had suggested she work in advertising, with paper pictures, she had excelled so quickly and so thoroughly that it seemed like her calling. *Security*. The wood is no more flammable than stone or brick, how to put it without suggesting the idea of a house fire. That's where all the tact and delicacy lie.

She gets up abruptly. Is Catherine crying tonight as well?

Louise is sleeping. Catherine is staring at the ceiling. Laurence goes to her.

— You're not sleeping, my darling? What are you thinking about?

— Nothing.

Laurence kisses her, concerned. Catherine isn't the mysterious type; she's open, even chatty.

— We're always thinking of *something*. Try to tell me.

Catherine hesitates a moment, then decides to trust her mother's smile.

— Maman, why do we exist?

This is exactly the kind of question that children assail you with, when all you're thinking about is how to sell wood panelling. Make this quick.

— My beloved, your father and I would be very sad if you didn't exist.

— But what if you didn't exist any more either?

Such anxiety from such a small girl, whom I still treat like a baby. Why is she asking this question? No wonder she's been crying.

— Weren't you happy this afternoon, that you, and me, and everybody existed?

— Yes.

Catherine seems unconvinced. Laurence has a flash of inspiration:

— We exist so that we can make each other happy, she says with a flourish. She is quite pleased with her response.

Catherine's face is unchanged. She goes on thinking, she seems to be looking for the right words.

— But what about people who are unhappy, why do they exist?

Now we're getting somewhere.

— Have you seen unhappy people? Where, my darling?

Catherine stops talking, and seems fearful. Where? Goya is happy and she hardly speaks French. The neighbourhood is wealthy, no tramps or beggars. So – books? School friends?

— Do you have friends at school who are unhappy?

— Oh no!

Her voice sounds sincere. Louise turns over in her bed, and it's time Catherine was asleep. She clearly doesn't want to say any more, and it will take time to help her sort this out.

— Listen, we can talk about this some more tomorrow. But if you know any unhappy people, we will try to do something for them. We can help look after the sick, give money to the poor, there are plenty of things we can do.

— You think so? For everybody?

— Don't you think I would cry all day if there were people who couldn't be helped at all? You'll tell me everything. And I promise we'll find something to do. I promise, she repeats, stroking Catherine's hair. Sleep now, my little love.

Catherine goes limp under the sheet, and closes her eyes. Her mother's voice, and her kisses, have calmed her. But tomorrow? Generally Laurence avoids reckless promises. And she's never before made such a rash one as this.

Jean-Charles looks up at her.

— Catherine was telling me about her dream, says Laurence. Tomorrow she'll tell him the truth. Not tonight. Why? He cares about the girls. Laurence sits down and pretends to be absorbed in her work. Not tonight. He'll immediately furnish five or six explanations. She wants to try to understand before he's had a chance to respond. What's wrong? I, too, cried when I was that age – how I cried! Maybe that's why I never cry now. Mlle Houchet used to say: *It is up to us to ensure that these deaths were not in vain.* I believed her. She always said so many things: to be a man among men! She died of cancer. The gas chambers, Hiroshima – there were many reasons why, in 1945, a child of eleven would feel completely stupefied. Laurence had even thought it was impossible that so much horror should have been for nothing; she tried to believe in God, in another life in which everything had its reward. Dominique had been perfect: she had allowed her to speak with a priest, she had even chosen an intelligent one. In '45, of course, it was normal. But today, if my ten-year-old daughter is crying, it's my fault, Dominique and Jean-Charles will blame me. She may even say I should take her to see a psychologist. Catherine reads a lot, too much, and I don't know exactly what, I don't have time. In any case, the words wouldn't mean the same thing to me as they do to her.

— Do you realise that in our very own galaxy there are hundreds of planets with life on them! says Jean-Charles, tapping his magazine with a thoughtful finger. We're like chickens who take our coop for the entire world.

— Oh, even on earth, we live cooped up in our narrow existence.

— Not today. With the print media, travel, television, soon international television, we live on a planetary level. The mistake is to take the planet for the universe. I mean, by 1985 we'll be exploring the solar system . . . Doesn't it sound like a dream come true?

— Frankly, no.

— You have no imagination.

I don't even know the people who live one floor up, thinks Laurence. The neighbours across the hall she knows a lot about, through the door: the bath runs, the doors slam, the radio spills out songs and ads for Banania, the husband yells at his wife who when he leaves goes and yells at their son. But what happens in the other 340 apartments in the building? In the other houses in Paris? At Publinf she knows Lucien, Mona a little, and a few faces and names. Family, friends: small, closed systems, and all these other systems are just as inaccessible. The world is always elsewhere, and there is no way of entering it. And yet it has slipped into Catherine's life, it scares her and I have to protect her from it. How to get her to accept that there are people who are less fortunate, how to make her believe that they will stop being that way?

— You're not tired? asks Jean-Charles.

But inspiration will not come tonight, there's no use fighting it. She models her smile on her husband's own:

— I'm tired.

Night-time rituals, the joyful noise of water in the bathroom, on the bed the pair of pyjamas which smells like lavender and blonde tobacco, and Jean-Charles smokes a cigarette while the shower washes away the cares of the day. Quick face wash, slip on a thin nightdress, she's ready. (What a first-rate invention the birth control pill is, you take it in the morning while you brush your teeth – no more having to mess around with a diaphragm.) Between the clean fresh sheets, the nightdress slips back off, floats over her head, she abandons herself to the softness of her body, naked. The playfulness of touching each other. A violent, joyful pleasure. After ten years of marriage, this complete physical understanding. Yes, but that doesn't change the flavour of life. Love is also smooth, hygienic, routine.

— Yes of course, your drawings are charming, says Laurence.

Mona really does have talent; she came up with a funny little figure that Laurence has often used in her campaigns, rather too often, says Lucien who specialises in customer motivation at the firm.

— But? says Mona. She is like her creature: clever, sharp and graceful.

— You know what Lucien always says. You can't rely on humour too much. And in this case – the wood is expensive, this is serious – the colour photographs do it more justice.

Laurence has chosen two, composed according to her instructions: a deep forest, thick with moss, mysterious, the old tree trunks faintly glowing; and a young woman, half-dressed in something filmy, smiling in the middle of a room decorated with wood panels.

— I think they're cheap, says Mona.

— Cheap, but eye-catching.

— I'm going to end up getting thrown out of this place. Drawing doesn't matter at all any more here. You always prefer photos.

She gathers up her sketches and asks, with curiosity:

— What's going on with Lucien? Are you no longer seeing him?

— Of course I am.

— You never ask me to cover for you any more.

— I will ask you at some point.

Mona leaves Laurence's office and Laurence goes back to tinkering with the text which will accompany the image. Her heart isn't in it. Behold the debased state of the female worker, she says to herself, ironically. (She felt even more debased before, when she didn't work.) At home, she tries to think up slogans. At work she thinks of Catherine. For three days she's hardly thought of anything else.

The conversation went on and on, becoming no clearer. Laurence asked herself what book, what encounter could have put Catherine in such a state; what the little girl had wanted to know was how to eliminate misfortune. Laurence had talked about social workers who help old people, and people living in poverty. About nurses, and doctors who heal the sick.

— Can I become a doctor?

— If you continue to work hard, of course.

Catherine's face lit up. They talked about her future: she would help children. Their mothers, too, but especially the children.

— What about you? What are you doing to help those less fortunate?

The merciless gaze of children who refuse to play the game.

— I help Papa support us. Thanks to me, you can go to school and cure the sick.

— And Papa?

— He builds houses for people who need them. That's also a way of helping them, you see?

(Horrible lie. But what truth can she tell?) Catherine remained bewildered. Why don't we give everyone food? Laurence had again asked questions and Catherine ended up talking about the poster. Because it was the most important thing or to hide something else?

Maybe the poster was the real explanation, after all: the power of the image. *Two thirds of the world go hungry*, and the face of the little boy, so beautiful, with big, big eyes and some terrible secret behind his closed lips. For me it's a sign: the sign that the struggle against hunger continues. But Catherine sees a little boy of about her age who is hungry. I remember well how grown-ups once seemed completely insensitive! There are so many things we don't notice. Well, we do notice, but we move on to other things because we know it's pointless to dwell on them. What use is a bad conscience? On this question, for once, Papa and Jean-Charles are in agreement. That story about the people being tortured, three years ago – I was positively sick over it, or almost. Where was the good in that? We are forced to get used to the horrors of the world, there are simply far too many of them:

force-feeding geese, genital mutilation, lynching, abortions, suicides, child martyrs, the death camps, the massacre of hostages, crackdowns, you see it at the cinema, on the television, you move on. It will disappear, it will have to, it's just a question of time. Except children live in the present, they have no defences. We should think of the children. We shouldn't put these kinds of photographs on the walls, Laurence says to herself. An abject thought. Abject: a word from when I was fifteen years old. But what does it mean? I'm reacting like any mother who wants to protect her daughter.

— Tonight, Papa will explain everything, Laurence says. Ten and a half: the age when a daughter should begin to detach herself a bit from her mother and start to fixate on her father. And he will be better able than I to find the appropriate arguments to satisfy her, she thought.

At the outset, Jean-Charles's tone annoys her. Not exactly ironic, or condescending, but rather – paternalistic. Then he makes a very clear, very convincing speech. Until recently, different places in the world had been very far apart, and men didn't know how to get by, and they were very selfish. This poster proves that we want things to change. Now we can produce much more food than before, and we can ship it quickly and easily from rich countries to poor ones – there are groups that take care of this. Jean-Charles waxes lyrical, as he does every time he pictures the future: the deserts will be covered with wheat, vegetables, fruit, the whole earth will become the promised land; children will smile, stuffed with milk, rice, tomatoes and oranges. Catherine listens, fascinated. She can see the orchards, and the fields in full bloom.

— In ten years, no one will be sad any more?

— We can't say that. But everyone will eat; everyone will be a lot happier.

Then she says, in a serious voice:

— I would have liked it better if I had been born ten years later.

Jean-Charles laughed, proud of his precocious daughter. He doesn't take her tears seriously, pleased with her success at school. Often children are disorientated, when they start secondary school; but she found Latin interesting, and had good grades in all her subjects. *We'll make someone of her*, Jean-Charles told me. Yes, but who? For the moment she's a child with a big heart and I don't know how to console her.

The telephone rings inside.

— Laurence? Are you alone?

— Yes.

— I'm calling in to say hello. He's going to scold me, Laurence thinks; it's true she's been neglecting him since school started back up. The house had to be reopened, Goya had to be brought up to date, Louise had bronchitis. Eighteen months since that party at Publinf where, as a matter of tradition, neither husbands nor wives are allowed. They danced a lot together (he is a very good dancer), they kissed, the miracle returned, the fire in the veins, the vertigo. They went back to his place, she didn't return home until morning, pretending to be drunk – although she hadn't touched a drop, she never drank – with no regrets because Jean-Charles would never find out and there wouldn't be a next time. Then – oh, the drama! He pursued me, he cried, I gave in, he left me, I suffered, I looked for his red Alfa Romeo everywhere, I waited by the phone, he came back, he begged me, leave your husband, no never, but I love you, he insulted me, he left again. I waited, I hoped, I despaired, we reunited, what happiness, I suffered so without you, and I without you, tell your husband everything, never. All this back and forth, always returning to the same point.

— I was just thinking I needed your opinion on something, says Laurence. Which one do you prefer?

Lucien leans over her shoulder. He examines the two photos; she is touched by how seriously he considers her question.

— Hard to say. They play to such different compulsions.

— Which is more efficient?

— I'm not aware of any convincing statistics. Trust your instincts.

He places a hand on Laurence's shoulder.

— When are we having dinner?

— Jean-Charles is going to Roussillon with Vergne in a little more than a week.

— More than a week!

— Come on! I'm having some trouble with my daughter just now.

— I don't see what that has to do with it.

— I do.

They've been down this conversational road; they know it too well. You don't want to see me any more, yes I do, try to understand, I understand all too well. (Is it possible that right this instant, in another part of the galaxy, another Lucien and another Laurence are saying the same things? They certainly are in offices, bedrooms and cafés across Paris, London, Rome, New York, Tokyo – maybe even in Moscow.)

— Let's have a drink tomorrow night after work. Will that do?

He looks at her reproachfully.

— You don't give me much of a choice.

He leaves angry. Too bad. He had made a real attempt to accept the situation. He knows she'll never divorce her husband and he doesn't threaten to leave any more. He gives in to everything, or almost. She cares about him; he provides a nice break from Jean-Charles, so different from him – water and fire. He likes novels that tell stories, memories of childhood, asking questions, going for long aimless walks. And then when he looks at her she feels like she's worth something. Worth something: she's letting herself be had, that's for certain. We think we care about a man, but it's actually just an idea of ourselves we can't let relinquish, an illusion of freedom, or spontaneity; a mirage. (Is that true? Or is the advertising business distorting my mind?) She finishes writing her text. Finally she opts for the young, vaporously half-dressed woman. She closes up her office, gets in the car. While she's putting on her gloves and changing her shoes, a feeling of joy rises within her. In her mind she is already in the apartment in the rue de l'Université, full of books and smelling strongly of cigarette smoke. Unfortunately she never stays long. She loves her father the most – more than anyone in the world – and she sees Dominique much more often. My whole life has been this way: it's my father I love, but my mother who made me.

— You oaf!

She hesitated half a second too long, that bastard slipped right into her spot. Back to driving round and around in these tiny one-way streets, where parking is bumper to bumper. Underground car parks, four-storey shopping centres, a technical city beneath the Seine riverbed – not for another ten years. I would also prefer to be living ten years in the future. A space! Finally! A hundred metres on foot later, and it's a different world: an old-fashioned caretaker's lodge, with a pleated curtain and the smell of something cooking, a quiet courtyard, a stone staircase to climb, on which every step echoes.

— It's getting more and more impossible to park.

— You took the words right out of my mouth.

With her father, even banalities are not banal, because of

the conspiratorial glint in his eyes. They share a taste for complicity: these moments when we feel as close to another person as if we lived only for one another. The glint of light returns when, after sitting her down and offering her a glass of orange juice, he asks:

— How is your mother?

— In excellent shape.

— Who is she imitating these days?

It's one of their old jokes, a question Freud asked about a hysteric. The fact is, Dominique is always imitating someone.

— I think just now it's Jacqueline Verdelet. She has the same hairdo and she's given up Cardin in favour of Balenciaga.

— She sees the Verdelets? That riff-raff? I suppose she's never had any scruples . . . Did you mention Serge to her?

— She doesn't want to do anything to help him.

— I thought as much.

— She doesn't seem to care very much for my uncle and aunt. She calls them Philemon and Baucis.

— That's not very accurate. I think my sister has lost most of her illusions about Bernard. She's no longer truly in love with him.

— What about him?

— He never truly appreciated her.

Truly in love; truly appreciated. For him these words have meaning. He truly loved Dominique. And who else? Who else is worthy of being loved by him? No one, no doubt, otherwise he wouldn't have that cynical wrinkle at the corner of his mouth.

— People are always surprising me, he goes on. Bernard is against the government but he thinks it's fine for his son to go and work for the ORTF, which is a government agency. I must be very old-fashioned: I have always tried to live my life in accordance with my principles.

— I don't have any principles, Laurence says with regret.

— You don't advertise them, but you're right-minded, it's better than the opposite, her father says warmly.

She laughs, takes a sip of orange juice, she feels good. What wouldn't she give for a bit of praise from him? Incapable of dishonour, of manipulation, indifferent to money. There's no one else like him.

He looks through his records. He doesn't have a fancy hi-fi, but he has many lovingly chosen records.

— I'm going to play something for you: a new recording of the *Couronnement de Poppée*.

Laurence tries to concentrate. A woman is bidding goodbye to her country, her friends. It's beautiful. She looks at her father. To be able to commune with herself, as he does. What she had thought she had seen in Jean-Charles, in Lucien, can actually only be found in him: on his face, a reflection of the infinite. To be a companion to oneself, to make a home that radiates warmth. I indulge in regret, I blame myself for neglecting him, when in fact I'm the one who needs him. She watches him, wondering what his secret is, and if she'll ever find out. She's not listening to the music. It's been a long time since it ceased to be meaningful to her. Monteverdi's pathos, or Beethoven's tragedy, speak of a kind of pain that she has never known: deep, ardent, mastered. She has known some bitter estrangements, a certain irritation, a certain desolation, disarray, emptiness, boredom, especially boredom. You don't sing about boredom.

— Yes, it's magnificent, she says in a fervent voice.

(*Say what you think*, Mlle Houchet used to say. Even with her father, it's impossible. We say what people expect us to.)

— I knew you would like it. Shall I play the next one?

— Not today. I wanted to ask your advice. About Catherine.

Immediately attentive and open, without a preconceived idea of how he will respond. When she's finished talking, he asks:

— Is everything all right between you and Jean-Charles?

An appropriate question. Maybe I wouldn't have cried so over the murdered Jewish children if there hadn't been such heavy silences in the house.

— Perfectly fine.

— You answered that awfully quickly.

— Really, everything is fine. I'm not as dynamic as he is, but, well, where the children are concerned, it all balances out. Unless I'm a bit distracted.

— Because of work?

— No. I just feel slightly distracted in general. But with the children no, I don't think so.

Her father is quiet. She asks:

— What can I tell Catherine?

— There's nothing to say. Once the question has been asked, there's no way to answer it.

— But I have to. Why do we exist? OK, it's abstract, it's metaphysical, the question doesn't worry me much. But unhappiness – that's so destructive for a child.

— Even in unhappiness we can find some joy. But I will admit it's not easy to explain to a ten-year-old girl.

— So?

— So I will try to talk with her, and to understand what's bothering her. Then I'll tell you.

Laurence gets up.

— We have to go, it's time.

Maybe Papa will be better at it than I am, or Jean-Charles, Laurence thinks to herself. He knows how to talk to children; he finds the right tone for everyone. And he invents the most charming gifts. When he arrives at the flat, he takes from his pocket a brightly striped cardboard cylinder, which looks like a giant stick of rock. One by one Louise, Catherine and Laurence are mesmerised by the enchantment of colours and shapes that form and re-form, dance and multiply in fugitive symmetry within an octagon. A kaleidoscope with nothing inside; the world itself fills in the rest, the dahlias, the rug, the curtains, the books. Jean-Charles eyes it, too.

— That would be very helpful for someone who designs textiles, or wallpaper, he says. They'd get ten ideas per minute.

Laurence serves soup, which her father swallows wordlessly. (*You're not eating, you're feeding yourself*, he said to her one day; she is as indifferent to culinary pleasures as Jean-Charles.) He tells the children stories which make them laugh and without seeming to ask them any questions, he interrogates them. It would be funny to walk on the Moon, would they be afraid to go there? No, not at all, if they were to go, they would know what they were doing, it would be no scarier than taking an aeroplane. They have not been at all impressed by the astronauts; on television they've found them kind of silly; they'd already read that story in comic books, they'd even read about a Moon landing, what they find surprising is that it hasn't happened yet. They would like to meet the men their father has told them about, those superhumans, those subhumans who live on other planets. They give detailed descriptions of them, interrupting one another, excited by the sounds their voices are making, their grandfather's presence, and the relatively ostentatious meal. Do they study astronomy at school? No. But we have fun, says Louise. Catherine talks about her friend Brigitte who is a year older than she is, she is so clever, and about her French teacher, who is a little stupid. Stupid, how? She says stupid things. We can't get her to say what. They stuff themselves with pineapple ice cream and beg their grandfather to take them one Sunday for a drive in the car, like he promised. To see the châteaux in the Loire, for example, the ones they've read about in history class?

— Laurence is worried about nothing, don't you think? Jean-Charles asks when the three of them are alone. At Catherine's age all intelligent children ask similar questions.

— But why those particular questions? says Laurence. She lives a very sheltered life.

— Whose life can be sheltered today, asks her father, with the newspapers, the television, the cinema?

— I'm very careful about what they watch on television, says Laurence. And we don't leave newspapers lying about.

She forbade Catherine to read the newspapers; she explained to her, with the help of examples, that when we are ignorant we are at risk of getting things wrong, and that the newspapers lie a great deal.

— You can't control everything. Do you know her new best friend?

— No.

— Tell her to bring her home. Try to get a sense of what they talk about.

— In any case Catherine is happy, she's healthy, and she works very hard. There is no reason to think a little bout of oversensitivity is anything to get upset about.

Laurence would like to think that Jean-Charles is right.

When she goes to kiss them goodnight, the little girls jump on their bed and turn somersaults, laughing riotously. She laughs with them, she tucks them in. But Catherine's anxious face returns to her. Who is Brigitte? Even if she has nothing to do with this, I still should have asked. Too many things are getting away from me.

She returns to the studio. Her father and Jean-Charles are having one of those discussions which sees them face off every Wednesday.

— No, no, men have not lost connection with their roots, says Jean-Charles. What's changed is that now they are rooted globally.

— They are no longer anywhere while at the same time being everywhere. We have never been so bad at travelling.

— You want travel to be disorientating. But the Earth has become just one big country. To such an extent that you find it surprising that it should take any time to get from one place to another. Jean-Charles looks at Laurence:

— Do you remember when we came back from New York last time? We've become so accustomed to air travel that a seven-hour flight seemed endless.

— Proust said the same thing about the telephone. Do you remember? When he called his grandmother, from Doncières. He said that the miracle of this faraway voice had become so familiar that waiting for it irritated him.

— I don't remember, says Jean-Charles.

— This generation of children think it's normal that we

should go for a stroll in space. Nothing surprises anyone any more. Soon we'll mistake technology for nature itself and we'll live in a perfectly inhuman world.

— Why inhuman? The face of mankind will be changed; we can't lock it up in some unchangeable idea. But during our leisure time we'll be able to reconnect with the values we hold dear: individualism, art.

— We're not headed that way.

— Yes, we are! Look at the decorative arts; look at architecture. We're no longer content with functionality. We've returned to a version of the Baroque, I mean to its aesthetic values.

And what good is that? thinks Laurence. Anyway, time will neither speed up nor slow down. Jean-Charles is already living in 1985, while Papa is nostalgic for 1925. At least he's talking about a world that existed, that he loved; Jean-Charles is inventing a future which may never come to pass.

— Admit that there is nothing uglier than the countryside covered in railway tracks, the way it used to be, he says. Now the SNCF and the EDF are making a real effort to respect natural sites of great beauty.

— A pitiful effort.

— Of course not.

Jean-Charles lists the train stations and the power stations that were in perfect harmony with their settings. In these arguments, he always has the upper hand because he can refer to facts. Laurence smiles at her father. He's decided to stop talking, but the spark in his eyes and the fold of his mouth indicate that he is strong in his convictions.

He's going to leave, Laurence thinks, and this time, too, she won't truly have taken advantage of his being there. What is wrong with me? My mind is always somewhere else.

— Your father really is the kind of man who refuses to join the twentieth century, Jean-Charles said an hour later.

— Whereas you live in the twenty-first, says Laurence with a smile.

She sits down at her table. She has to examine some recent studies Lucien conducted; she opens the file. It's fastidious, even depressing work. Smoothness, brilliance, lustre, dreams of gliding, of glazed perfection; erotic values and childhood values (innocence); speed, domination, heat, security. Can everyone's preferences be explained by such basic fantasies? Or were the consumers interviewed particularly slow? Unlikely. These psychologists have a thankless job to do. Endless questionnaires, attempts at fine-tuning, trick questions, and we always end up with the same answers. People want novelty, but without risk; things that are entertaining, while still serious; social status, without having to pay too much for it. For her, it's always the same problem: how to arouse and surprise while also reassuring; the magic product which will completely change our lives without disturbing them at all. She asks:

— Did you ask a lot of questions when you were little?

— I suppose so.

— You don't remember what they were?

— No.

He goes back to reading his book. He claims to have forgotten everything about his childhood. A father with a small factory in Normandy, two brothers, normal relationship with his mother – no reason to try to escape his past. But he never talks about it.

He reads. Since the file is so boring she thinks she might read, too. But what? Jean-Charles loves books about nothing. You know, what is so amazing about these young writers is that they don't write to tell a story; they write to write, the way we would stack rocks on top of each other, just for the pleasure of it. She started reading a description, in three hundred pages, of a suspension bridge; she didn't last ten minutes. As for the novels Lucien recommends, they're always about people and events as far removed from her life as Monteverdi.

So. Literature doesn't mean much to me any more. But I should try to learn. I've become so ignorant! Papa said: *Laurence will be a bookworm like me.* And instead of that . . . That she should have regressed in the early years of her marriage is unsurprising. Classic. Love, motherhood, it's a violent emotional shock, when you marry quite young, and she could never find a balance between intelligence and affection. It seemed as if I no longer had a future. Jean-Charles did, and the girls, but not me. So what was the point of cultivating my mind? It was a vicious circle: I neglected myself, I was bored and I felt more and more dispossessed of myself. (And, of course, her depression had deeper causes, but she didn't need a psychoanalyst to get out of it; she found a career which interested her, and she got better.) And now? The problem is different. I don't have enough time; having to find ideas and write slogans verges on obsession. All the same, soon after she started at Publinf she at least read the newspaper; now she relies on Jean-Charles to keep her up to date. It's not enough. *Make your own opinions!* Mlle Houchet used to say. She would be so disappointed if she saw me today! Laurence picks up a copy of *Le Monde* that's been left on a side table. It's discouraging. You can't lose the thread of what's going on, or you'll drown – everything has already begun beforehand. What is Burundi? and OCAM? Why are the Buddhist priests unhappy? Who is General Delgado? Where exactly is Ghana? She refolds the newspaper, relieved, because you never know what you might see in there. I was right to shield myself, I'm not as strong as they are. *Women's nervous tendencies*, says Jean-Charles, who is, nevertheless, a feminist. I fight it: I can't stand my neuroses, so it's better to avoid things that might set them off.

She returns to the file. Why do we exist? Not my problem. We exist. You just have to try not to notice it, to get a running start and then jump off into the air, sailing right through it, until the end. I broke off in mid-air five years ago. I bounced right back. But life is so long. We keep falling down. My problem is this decline as you get closer and closer, as if there were indeed an answer to Catherine's question, a terrifying one. No! Just thinking about it brings me closer to neurosis. I won't fall again. Now I'm forewarned, I'm forearmed, I have myself in check. And anyway, I'm well aware of the real reasons for my breakdown. I'm not ignoring them, I've moved past them. I articulated the conflict between my feelings for Jean-Charles and those I have for my father, it no longer torments me. I have squared up with myself.

The children are sleeping, Jean-Charles is reading. Somewhere Lucien is thinking of her. She feels her life around her, full, warm, like a nest, a cocoon. All that's needed is a bit of vigilance to keep any cracks from appearing, and threatening this security.

2

Why does Gilbert want to see me? Set back in their damp gardens which smell of autumn and the country, all the houses in Neuilly look like clinics. *Don't tell Dominique.* There was fear in his voice. Was it cancer? or heart trouble?

— Thank you for coming.

Greys and reds in perfect harmony, black carpet, rare books on shelves made of the finest wood, two modern paintings with expensive signatures, the hi-fi, the bar – her job is to sell this kind of millionaire's study to each customer for the price of a length of fabric or a shelf made of pitch pine.

— Whisky?

— No thank you. Her throat is dry. What's going on?

— Juice?

— Yes please.

He pours for her, he pours for himself, he puts ice cubes in his glass, he's taking his time. Because he is accustomed to being in charge and only speaking when he's good and ready? Or is he uncomfortable?

— You know Dominique so well – you'll be able to give me some advice.

Her heart, or cancer. For Gilbert to be asking Laurence's advice, it has to be serious. The words he pronounces hang in the air, stripped of all meaning:

— I'm in love with a young woman.

— What do you mean?

— In love. As in *in love*. With a young lady of nineteen.

His mouth takes the shape of a smile and he speaks in a paternal voice, as if he were explaining some basic truth to someone very simple-minded.

— It's not that uncommon these days for a nineteen-year-old girl to love a man who's over fifty.

— Because she's in love with you too?

— Yes.

No! cries Laurence wordlessly. Maman! my poor Maman! She does not want to interrogate Gilbert, she does not want to help him explain himself.

He is silent. She lacks the strength to hold out; she gives in.

— So?

— So we're going to get married.

This time she cries aloud:

— But that's impossible!

— Marie-Claire accepted the divorce. She knows Patricia and likes her very much.

— Patricia?

— Yes. The daughter of Lucile de Saint-Chamont.

— That's impossible! Laurence repeats.

She saw Patricia once, a girl of twelve, blonde and well-mannered; and her photograph the previous year at the debutante ball. A lovely little idiot, with no money at all, pushed by her mother into the arms of wealthy men.

— You can't leave Dominique. It's been seven years!

— My point exactly.

His voice turns cynical and his pout turns into a smile. He is, quite simply, a cad. Laurence feels her heart speed up, fast, very fast. She is living through one of those nightmares where you can't tell if things are really happening to you or if you're watching an upsetting film. Marie-Claire accepted the divorce, of course, she's only too happy to do Dominique a bad turn.

— But Dominique loves you. She thought you'd be together till the end. She won't be able to bear being abandoned.

— We bear up though, don't we.

Laurence is quiet, it's useless to say anything and she knows it.

— Come on, don't take that put-out air. Your mother will bounce back. She knows very well that a fifty-one-year-old woman is much older than a fifty-six-year-old man. She has her career, her social life, that will help her through it. I'm just asking, and this is what I wanted to speak to you about, what might be the best way to present the situation to her.

— All the ways are bad.

Gilbert looks at Laurence with that charming expression which has given him such a reputation:

— I have great confidence in your judgement. In your opinion, should I only say I no longer love her, or tell her about Patricia right away?

— She won't be able to bear it. Please don't do this! Laurence begs.

— I will speak to her tomorrow afternoon. Clear your diary so you can see her at the end of the day. She will need someone. Call me to let me know how she's reacted.

— No! says Laurence.

— The idea is to hurt her as little as possible; I would even like to remain friends. It's for her own good.

Laurence gets up and walks towards the door. He catches her by the arm.

— Do not speak to her about this conversation.

— I'll do as I like.

Behind her, Gilbert is murmuring banalities, she doesn't extend her hand to him, she slams the door, she hates him. It's a relief to suddenly be able to say *I have always loathed Gilbert*. As she walks she crushes dead leaves beneath her feet and around her fear is thick as fog. But the brightness and solidity of this realisation pierces the shadows: I hate him! and she thinks: Dominique will hate him! She is proud, she is strong.

We don't behave like a simpering little shop girl. It will hurt, but her pride will save her. A difficult but noble role to play, the woman who elegantly bears her abandonment. She will throw herself into work, she will take another lover . . . What if I went to warn her myself, now, right away? Laurence sits, without moving, at the wheel of her car. She has broken out in a sweat, she wants to vomit. Dominique cannot be told what Gilbert wants to tell her. Something will happen, he'll die during the night, or she will. Or there'll be an earthquake.

It's tomorrow, and there's been no earthquake. Laurence parks on a pedestrian crossing, too bad if she gets a ticket. She's called three times from the office and each time the line was engaged. Dominique has the phone off the hook. She takes the lift, she wipes her sweaty hands. Try to be normal.

— Am I disturbing you? I tried to reach you on the phone, but couldn't get through. I need some advice.

She's clearly lying, she never asks her mother for advice, but Dominique has barely heard her.

— Come in.

They sit down in the *relaxation corner* of the large salon, lushly decorated in muted tones. In a vase sits an enormous bouquet of sharp yellow flowers which look like aggressive birds. Dominique's eyes are puffy. Has she been crying? Sounding almost triumphant, she announces:

— I have a good one for you!

— What is it?

— Gilbert has just informed me that he's in love with another woman.

— Are you joking? Who?

— He didn't say. He just explained that we had to *shift our relationship to another level*. What a phrase! He won't be coming to Feuverolles this weekend. Her voice turns mocking. He's dumped me! But I will find out who this person is and I promise you, it won't go well for them!

Laurence hesitates. Perhaps it's time to rip off the plaster? Her heart isn't in it, she's afraid. Play for time.

— It's probably just a whim.

— Gilbert has never had whims, he only has will. Suddenly she bellows. *Bastard! The complete bastard!*

Laurence takes her mother by the shoulders.

— Don't cry.

— I will cry as much as I like. He's a bastard, a bastard!

Laurence would never have believed her mother could cry like this, that anyone could cry like this, it was like bad theatre. Onstage, OK, but for real, in real life? Her voice climbs higher, sharper, indecent in the luxury of this relaxation corner. – You bastard, you bastard!

(In another salon, completely different, exactly the same, with vases full of ostentatious flowers, the same cry comes from another mouth. *You bastard!*)

Dominique collapses on the sofa in tears.

— You don't understand. He does this to me? Dumps me like a shop girl?

— You didn't suspect anything?

— Nothing. He really had me going. You saw him the other weekend, he was all smiles.

— What did he say, exactly?

Dominique sits up, runs her fingers through her hair, tears on her face.

— That he owed it to me to tell me the truth. He values me, he admires me, the usual nonsense. But he loves someone else.

— You didn't ask her name?

— I got it wrong, says Dominique between her teeth. She wipes her eyes. I can just hear what they'll say. Gilbert Mortier has dumped Dominique. How they'll crow over it!

— Find someone else. There are enough men falling over you.

— Tell me about it. Little social climbers.

— Go on a trip, show them you don't need him. You're completely right, he's a bastard. Do what you have to do to get over him.

— That would make him all too happy, are you joking? That's exactly what he wants.

She gets up, walks around the room.

— I'll get him back. One way or another. She has a nasty look in her eyes. He was my last chance, do you understand me?

— Of course not.

— Come on! You don't make a new life at fifty-one.

She says again, maniacally:

— I will get him back! By force if necessary.

— By force?

— If I can find a way to put pressure on him.

— How?

— I'll work something out.

— But what good is he to you if you have to force him to be there?

— He'd be there. I wouldn't be a jilted woman.

She sits down again, her gaze fixed, her mouth tight. Laurence speaks. She pronounces words she has gathered from her mother's lips: *preserve your dignity, your serenity, take courage, keep your self-respect, look happy, conduct yourself with decorum, play the heroine.* Dominique doesn't answer. She finally says, exhausted:

— Go home. I need to think. Be a dear and telephone Pétridès to say I have a sore throat.

— Will you be able to sleep?

— Well, I'm not about to swallow a bottle of sleeping pills, if that's what you're worried about.

She takes Laurence's hands, an unusual gesture, it's awkward. Her fingers close around her wrists.

— Try to find out who this woman is.

— I don't know anyone in Gilbert's circle.

— Try anyway.

Laurence slowly goes downstairs. Something convulses in her chest and keeps her from breathing. She would rather be feeling overcome by tenderness and sadness. But she can still hear her mother's cry, see that nasty look in her eyes. Rage and wounded vanity, the harrowing pain of lost love, except without the love. Who could really be in love with Gilbert? And Dominique, had she ever been in love? Can she love? (He paced the room like an afflicted soul, he loved her, he still loved her. And Laurence was overcome with sadness and tenderness. And ever since there has hovered around Dominique a kind of evil glow.) Even her suffering doesn't humanise her. It's like hearing the rasp of a lobster, an inarticulate noise, signifying nothing, except for simple bare pain. More intolerable than if it could be shared.

I tried not to hear it, but the lobsters were rasping in my ears when I arrived home. Louise was beating eggs into a fluff in the kitchen while Goya looked on; I kissed her.

— Is Catherine home?

— She's in her bedroom, with Brigitte.

They were sitting facing each other in the dark. I turned on the light, Brigitte got up.

— Bonjour, m'dame.

Straight away I noticed the large safety-pin in the button-hole of her skirt: a motherless child, Catherine had told me. Tall, thin, with chestnut hair, short and unkempt, a faded blue jumper. She'd be quite pretty if someone looked after her. The room was a shambles; chairs overturned, cushions on the ground.

— Nice to meet you.

I kissed Catherine.

— What are you playing?

— We're talking.

— In this mess?

— Oh, Louise was here before and we were playing around.

— We'll tidy up, said Brigitte.

— No rush.

I set an armchair to rights and sat down. I didn't care if they ran and jumped and knocked over the furniture, but what were they talking about when I came in?

— What were you talking about?

— Nothing, just talking. Standing before me, Brigitte examined me, without impudence, just curiosity. I was slightly uncomfortable. Adults never really look at each other. Whereas those eyes really saw me. I picked up the copy of *Don Quixote* – abridged and illustrated – that Catherine had lent to her friend.

— You finished it? Did you like it? Sit down, won't you? She sat down.

— I haven't finished it.

She gave me a very pretty smile, not at all childish and even a little flirtatious.

— I get bored if a book is too long. And also I prefer true stories.

— Stories from history?

— Yes. And travel, and what you can read in the newspapers.

— Your father lets you read the newspapers?

She seemed startled. Hesitantly, she murmured:

— Yes.

Papa is right, I thought, I can't control everything. If she brings the newspapers to school, if she talks about what she's read in them – all those horrible stories, children being killed, drowned by their own mothers.

— Do you understand it all?

— My brother explains it to me.

Her brother is at university, her father is a doctor. Alone with two men. They must not look after her very much. Lucien claims that girls with older brothers mature faster than the others. That must be how she already has the manners of a young woman.

— What do you want to do when you grow up? Do you have any plans?

They looked at each other with a complicit air.

— I will be a doctor. She's going to be an agronomist.

— An agronomist? Do you like nature?

— My grandfather says that the future depends on agronomists.

I didn't dare ask her who her grandfather was. I looked at my watch. Quarter to eight.

— Catherine has to get ready for dinner. They're probably expecting you at home.

— Oh, we eat when we like at home, she said, with a casual air. Probably no one else is home yet.

Yes, her situation was clear. A neglected little girl who'd learned to be self-sufficient. She was neither allowed nor denied anything. She was growing up however she could. How young Catherine appeared by comparison! It would have been nice to invite her to stay to dinner. But Jean-Charles hated spontaneity. And, I don't know why, but I didn't really want him to meet Brigitte.

— Still, it's time for you to be going home. But wait, I'm going to sort out your skirt.

Her ears went red.

— Oh! It's no big deal.

— Yes it is, it's an eyesore.

— I'll sew it up when I get back.

— Let me at least fix the pin.

I did so, and she smiled at me.

— How kind you are!

— I would like for us to get to know each other. Would you like to come along to the Musée de l'Homme on Thursday, with Catherine and Louise?

— Oh! Yes!

Catherine guided Brigitte to the door; they whispered and laughed. I would have liked to sit down in the dark with a little girl when I was that age, and laugh and whisper. But Dominique always said: *I'm sure she's very nice, your little friend, but my poor girl, she's so ordinary.* Marthe had a friend, the daughter of one of Papa's friends, thick and dumb. But me, no. Never.

— Your friend is very nice.

— We have fun together.

— Does she get good marks?

— Oh yes, the best.

— Yours have fallen somewhat this month. Are you tired?

— No.

I didn't push it.

— She's older than you, that's why she's allowed to read the newspapers. But remember what I told you: you're too young.

— I remember.

— And you don't disobey?

— No.

I heard reluctance in her voice.

— You don't sound convinced.

— Of course I am. It's just that, you know, it's not difficult to understand what Brigitte tells me.

I felt annoyed. I liked Brigitte. But was she a good influence on Catherine?

— It's funny to want to be an agronomist. Do you understand it?

— I'd rather be a doctor. I'll heal the sick and she'll grow wheat and tomatoes in the desert and everyone will have enough to eat.

— Did you show her the poster with the hungry little boy?

— She's the one who showed it to me.

Obviously. I sent her to wash her hands and tidy her hair, and I went into Louise's room. She was sitting at her desk, drawing. It took me back. The dark room, with only a small lamp lit, the multicoloured crayons, a long day behind me studded with little pleasures, and the world outside, immense and mysterious. Precious moments, lost for ever. For them too, one day; they too will be for ever lost. What a pity! Keep them from growing up. Otherwise . . . what would happen?

— That's a lovely drawing, sweetheart.

— You can have it.

— Thank you. I will put it on the table. Did you have a good time with Brigitte?

— She taught me some dances. Louise's voice turned sad. But then they kicked me out.

— They had things to talk about. And that way you could help Goya with dinner. Papa will be so proud when he hears you made the soufflé almost completely by yourself.

She laughed, and then we heard the key turning in the lock. She ran to see her father.

That was yesterday. And now Laurence is worried. She sees Brigitte's smile again – *How kind you are!* – and tenderness comes over her. This friendship could be good for Catherine; she's old enough to be interested in what's happening in the world; I don't speak to her enough and her father intimidates her; it's just important she not be traumatised. Brigitte's maternal grandparents live in Israel, she spent the previous year with them, that's why she fell behind in her studies. Did she lose members of her family? All the horrors I sobbed over, has she told Catherine about them? I have to be careful, keep on top of things, I have to be the one who tells her. Laurence tries to concentrate on *France-Soir*. Another horrible story. A twelve-year-old who's hanged himself in prison. He asked for bananas, a towel, and he hanged himself. *Collateral damage*. Gilbert explained that in every society there was necessarily going to be collateral damage. Of course. Nevertheless Catherine would find this story very upsetting.

Gilbert: *Love, as in* in love. What a bastard! *Bastard, bastard*, Dominique cried in the relaxation corner. That morning, on the telephone, she said in a dull voice that she had slept well, and she hung up very quickly. What can I do for her? Nothing. It's so rare that we can actually do something for someone . . . For Catherine, yes. So do it. Work out how to answer her questions, and even how to pre-empt them. Help her find out about the real world without scaring her. To do that I need to be informed as well. Jean-Charles criticises me for being uninterested in my century; I should ask him to recommend books, and to make sure I read them. It's not a completely new idea. Occasionally Laurence makes these resolutions, but — why exactly? — she never really intends to keep them. This time it's different. It's about Catherine. If she failed her she would never forgive herself.

— It's good to have you here, says Lucien.

Laurence is sitting, wrapped in a dressing gown, in a leather armchair. He sits at her feet, also wearing a dressing gown, his face lifted to hers.

— I feel good being here.

— I want you to always be here.

They had made love, had a light meal, talked a bit, made love again. She is happy in this room; there is a sofa bed covered with a fur throw, a table, two leather armchairs bought at the flea market, a few books on some shelves, a telescope, a wind rose, a sextant. In a corner stood a pair of skis and pigskin suitcases. It was casual, nothing fancy, but it was also unsurprising to find such an abundance of elegant clothing in the wardrobe — suede jackets, cashmere sweaters, scarves, slippers. Lucien parts Laurence's robe and caresses her knee.

— You have such pretty knees. They're so rare, pretty knees.

— You have beautiful hands.

He is less well built than Jean-Charles, too thin; but his hands are delicate and strong, his face expressive, sensitive, and his gestures have a sinuous grace. The world he inhabits is hushed, all nuances and half-tones, chiaroscuro, whereas with Jean-Charles it is always high noon, a crude, equalising light.

— Do you want something to drink?

— No, but you go ahead.

He pours a glass of bourbon *on the rocks*, from a brand that is apparently hard to find. He doesn't care much about food, but he fancies himself a connoisseur when it comes to alcohol and wine. He settles back down at Laurence's feet.

— I bet you've never been drunk.

— I don't like alcohol.

— You don't like it or you're afraid?

She strokes his black hair, which is still as soft as a child's.

— Don't play psychologist with me.

— It's just that you're such a sweet little thing, but so difficult to understand. Sometimes so young, so cheerful, so close; other times, like Athena, armed for war.

At the beginning, she had liked it when he talked to her about herself. All women do. On this point Jean-Charles had never indulged her. But essentially, it's just idle talk. She knew too well what intrigued Lucien, or rather what unsettled him.

— Oh go on. It all depends on my hairdo.

He lays his head on her knees.

— Indulge me for five minutes, so I can imagine that

we'll stay this way all our lives. We'll go grey without notic-
ing. You'll be an adorable little old lady.

— Go right ahead, my darling.

Why does he say such stupid things? Love without end –
it's like that song, *it doesn't exist, it doesn't exist*. But that nostalgic
voice brings something back to her, like a blurry echo of
something she'd once lived through, on another planet. It is as
insinuating and pernicious as perfume, at night, in a closed
room – the scent of narcissus. She says, somewhat coldly:

— You'll tire of me.

— Never.

— Don't be romantic.

— An old doctor poisoned himself the other day, holding hands with his wife, who'd been dead for a week. It can
happen.

— Yes, but for what reasons? she asked, laughing.

He says, reproachfully:

— I'm not laughing.

She has allowed the conversation to take a stupidly senti-
mental turn and now it won't be easy to leave.

— I don't like to think about the future; the present is
enough, she says, pressing her hand to Lucien's cheek.

— Is that true? He looks at her. In his eyes, her own
image shines back at her, almost unbearably. Are you getting
bored of me?

— What an idea! There's no one who bores me less.

— That's a strange answer.

— Well, you're asking strange questions. Do I seem bored tonight?

— No.

Lucien's conversation is amusing. Together they talk about all the people at work, about their clients, they make up little stories about them. Or Lucien talks about novels he's read, places he's been, he knows how to find the precise detail to awaken in Laurence a fleeting desire to read, to travel. Before he was talking about Fitzgerald, whose name she had heard in passing, and she was astonished to hear that such an implausible story was real.

— It's been a perfect evening, she says.

He flinches.

— Why do you say *it's been*? It's not over.

— It's two a.m. My darling, I really must be going.

— What? You're not going to sleep here?

— The children are too big now, it's getting dangerous.

— Please?

— No.

Last year, when Jean-Charles was in Morocco, she'd often said *no*. She left and then she'd suddenly stop the car, turn around, and go running back up the stairs. He held her tightly. *You've come back to me!* And she would stay, until dawn. Because of the joy on his face. Today she won't come back. And he knows it.

— So that's it. You won't sleep here any longer.

She tenses. He has persuaded himself that when Jean-Charles isn't home, she'll stay with him. But she didn't promise anything.

— What if my daughters found out? The risk is too great.

— And yet you took that risk last year.

— I regretted it.

They stand up. He paces the room, stops in front of her, furious.

— Always the same old story. A little adultery here and there, but otherwise a good wife, a good mother. Why is there no word for *bad lover*, *bad mistress*? His voice catches, a troubled look comes over him. That means we'll never spend the night together again. The opportunity won't present itself.

— Maybe it will.

— No, because you won't let it. You don't love me any more, admit it.

— Then why am I here?

— You don't love me the way you did before. Since you came back from holiday it hasn't been the same.

— I promise you it has. We've had this very fight a hundred times before. Let me get dressed.

He pours another drink while she goes to the bathroom, where the shelves are covered in bottles and jars. Lucien collects the lotions and creams he receives as a gift from their clients at work, because it amuses him but also because he takes meticulous care of his appearance. Of course. I would stifle my feelings of remorse, if it could be the way it had been; the lightning-bolt infatuation, the burning nights, the whirlwinds and floods of desire, and pleasure – for these kinds of transformations you could say anything, betray anyone, risk it all. But for this friendly petting? For a pleasure so similar to what she gets with Jean-Charles? The mellowed-out emotions? It's all just a part of the daily grind. Even adultery can become mechanical, she thinks. The quarrels which once so excited her now tire her out. When she returns to the bedroom, he has finished his second glass.

— I understand. Go on. You were curious, you wanted a fling, because after all someone who hasn't cheated on their husband must be a wet blanket. But it was nothing more than that for you. And there I was, like an idiot, going on and on about eternal love.

— That's not true. She gets close to him, kisses him. I really care about you, quite strongly.

— Quite strongly! You've only ever given me crumbs. I resigned myself to it. But if your intention is to give me less even than that, it's better to end things.

— I give what I can.

— You can't hurt your husband, or your girls, but you have no trouble making me suffer.

— I don't want you to suffer.

— Oh come on, you don't care at all. I thought you were different from the others. At times it was almost as though

· 64 ·

you had a heart. But no. Who needs a heart when you can be so fashionable, a successful, independent woman?

He just keeps talking and talking. When Jean-Charles is upset, he clams up. Lucien talks. Two different approaches. It's true that as a child I learned to discipline my heart. Is that a good thing or not? Pointless to wonder; we can't change who we are.

— You don't drink, you never lose your cool, I've never seen you cry even once, you're afraid of losing yourself in something, or someone. That's what I call a refusal of life.

It feels as though she's been hit, though she can't tell where the wound is.

— What can I do. I am what I am.

He grabs her by the wrist.

— Do you understand? For a month, I've been waiting for these nights. Every night I've dreamed about them.

— OK, I was wrong! I should have let you know sooner.

— You didn't! So stay.

She delicately extricates herself from his grip.

— Think about it. If Jean-Charles suspected anything, it would be impossible to go on.

— Because you would give me up?

— Not this again.

— No. I know that I've lost.

Lucien's face softens; all that remains in his eyes is a great sadness.

— Well then, see you tomorrow.

— See you tomorrow. We'll have a beautiful evening together.

She kisses him, but he doesn't return it. He looks at her with sadness.

She doesn't feel pity; rather, as she walks back to her car, a kind of enviousness. She suffered that night in Le Havre, when he said he would rather stop right away. That was at the very beginning of their relationship, she was doing sales research on Mokeski coffee and he had gone with her. Having to organise himself around her husband and children, all the waiting around, the lying – he wasn't interested. *I'm going to lose him.* She felt a stabbing pain as precise as a physical injury. And again last winter when she came back from Chamonix. These two weeks have been torture, Lucien told her; it was better to end it altogether. She had begged him; he refused to give in. He didn't speak to her for ten days, ten hellish days, that bore no resemblance to the kind of pain they sing about in songs. It was sordid – furred mouth, constant nausea. But at least there was something to be sad about, something in the world that was worth its weight in pain. He still has this fever, and hopelessness, and hope. He's luckier than I am.

Why Jean-Charles rather than Lucien? Laurence asks herself, staring at her husband who is spreading orange marmalade on to a piece of toast. She knows full well that Lucien will forget her, and fall in love with someone else. (Why me rather than someone else?) She accepts it, and even, on some level, wishes it. It's just that she wonders – why Jean-Charles? The children left for Feuverolles the previous evening with Marthe, the apartment is quiet. But the neighbours are taking advantage of it being Sunday to bang like mad on the walls. Jean-Charles strikes the table.

— I can't stand it! I'm going to go and smash their heads in!

Since he's been back he's been bad-tempered, snapping at the children, losing his temper at Goya, rehashing his grievances.

— Vergne is a genius, a visionary, but so intransigent that in the end he never accomplishes anything. Dufrène was right. The contractor didn't accept his plans without changes, but still, he should have spared a thought for his colleagues before dropping the entire project. A whole fortune has slipped through our fingers. I'm going to try to get in with Monnod.

— You said you were building a fantastic team, that everyone was driven and enthusiastic.

— We can't eat enthusiasm. I'm worth more than I'm making with Vergne. At Monnod's I'd make double at least.

— Still, we live very well as it is.

— We'd live even better.

Jean-Charles had made his mind up to leave Vergne, who had been so good to him (what would have become of us when Catherine was born, without the cash he advanced us?), but first he wanted to verbally tear him to shreds.

— Incredible ideas, everyone's talking about them, the newspapers are full of them, it all sounds very nice, but in the end . . .

Why Jean-Charles rather than Lucien? She felt the same abyss widen inside her when she was with them both; it's just that with Jean-Charles there were solid bonds – the children, the future, the home – whereas with Lucien, when feeling had left her, she found herself before a stranger. But what if it had been him she had married? It would have been the same, neither better nor worse, or so it seemed to her. Why one man rather than another? How strange. We can find ourselves entangled for life with someone just because we met them when we were nineteen. She doesn't regret that it was Jean-Charles, far from it. So lively, so animated, full of ideas and projects, passionate about what he does, brilliant, kind to everyone. And faithful, loyal, a beautiful body, happy to make love often and well. He loves his house, his children and Laurence. In a different way than Lucien, less romantically, but solidly, tenderly. He needs her presence and her approval – if she appears to him sad or merely preoccupied, he worries. The ideal husband. She is proud of herself for having married him, him and not someone else, but all the same she is surprised something so important could be so random. No justifiable reason for it. (But everything is like that.) People talk about soulmates, but do you really find that anywhere apart from in books? Even the old doctor whose death was brought on by his wife's demise – that doesn't prove they were made for each other. *True love*, says Papa. Do I truly love Jean-Charles? or Lucien? She feels as if people are merely placed beside her, they don't live within her, except for her daughters, but that's how it should be.

— A great architect knows how to be flexible.

The doorbell interrupts Jean-Charles; he unfolds a panel, dividing the room in two, and Laurence brings Mona into her office in the corner.

— It's sweet of you to have come.

— I wasn't going to leave you in the lurch.

Mona is adorable in her trousers and oversized jumper, with her boyish figure, her girlish smile, and the graceful turn of her neck. Usually she refuses to lift so much as a finger outside office hours – we're exploited enough as it is. But the project has to be submitted by tonight at the latest and she knows very well that her mock-up isn't quite right. She looks around her.

— My goodness, you live in such style! She reflects a moment. I suppose between you both you must bring in a pretty penny.

No irony or reproach; she's comparing. She does fairly well for herself, but it seems – she doesn't speak of herself very often – that she comes from a modest background and that she has her whole family to support. She sits down beside Laurence and spreads her drawings out on the work table.

— I made a few different ones, with small variations.

Launching a new brand for a product as widely available as tomato sauce is no easy thing. Laurence had suggested that Mona play with a contrast between sunshine and coolness. The page she'd created was pleasant: lively colours, a sunny sky, a village on a hill, olive trees, and in the foreground, a can with the brand's label on it, and a tomato. But something is missing. The taste of the fruit, its flesh. They had talked it over at great length, and decided that they needed to make a notch in the skin, and reveal a bit of its interior.

— Oh! That makes all the difference, says Laurence. It makes you want to bite into it.

— Yes, I knew you'd be happy, says Mona. Look at the rest of them.

From one sheet to the next there were subtle changes of colour and shape.

— It's hard to choose one.

Jean-Charles walks into the room, his teeth shining, very white, and he shakes Mona's hand with enthusiasm.

— Laurence has told me so much about you! And I've seen so many of your drawings. Your Méribel was delightful. You are so talented.

— We do what we can, says Mona.

— Which of these drawings makes you crave tomato sauce? asks Laurence.

— They all look alike, no? Very pretty, too – like little paintings.

Jean-Charles rests his hand on Laurence's shoulder.

— I'm going to go and give the car a polish. Will you be ready at half past twelve? We can't leave much later than that if we want to make it to Feuverolles in time for lunch . . .

— I'll be ready.

He leaves, smiling.

— Are you going to the country? asks Mona.

— Yes, Maman has a house. We go nearly every Sunday. It's a good way to unwind . . .

She was going to say, out of habit, *absolutely necessary*, but she caught herself in time. She can hear Gilbert's voice: *an absolutely necessary way to unwind*, she looks at Mona's tense face, she feels vaguely ashamed. (No shame, no bad conscience, no gloomy pleasures.)

— It's funny, says Mona.

— What?

— It's funny how much your husband looks like Lucien.

— Are you joking? Lucien and Jean-Charles are apples and oranges.

— To me they're two peas in a pod.

— I really don't see what you mean.

— The kind of men with beautiful manners and white

teeth who know how to make small talk, who slap on the aftershave when they're finished shaving.

— Oh! If that's what you mean . . .

— That's what I mean. She abruptly changes the subject. So? Which one do you prefer?

Laurence studies them again. OK, Lucien and Jean-Charles wear aftershave. And what kind of man does Mona prefer? She would like to get her talking, but she's clammed up in a way that intimidates Laurence. How will she spend her Sunday?

— I think this one is the best. Because of the village, I like how the houses spill down the side of the hill . . .

— Me too, I prefer that one, says Mona. She puts her papers away. OK. I'm off.

— You don't want a drink? Some wine, or whisky? Or a tomato juice?

They laugh.

— No thank you, I'm fine. But show me where you live.

Mona goes from room to room, saying nothing. Sometimes she touches some upholstery, a wooden table. In the sun-drenched living room, she lets herself collapse into a wing chair.

— I can see why you don't understand anything at all.

Usually Mona is amicable, but sometimes it seems as though she detests Laurence. Laurence doesn't like to be detested, in general, and by Mona in particular. She gets up, and as she buttons her jacket she looks around one more time, in a way Laurence finds difficult to decode. In any case it's not out of jealousy.

Laurence walks her to the lift, and then returns to her table. She slips the chosen design along with the text she's written into an envelope, and feels somehow vexed. The disdain in Mona's voice. What is the source of her evident feelings of superiority? She isn't a communist, but all the same she must adhere to some proletarian doctrine, like Jean-Charles says; there is something sectarian in her, and it's not the first time Laurence has noticed it. (*If there's one thing I hate*, said Papa, *it's sectarianism.*) Too bad. That's why everyone stays in their own circles. If everyone tried a little bit, really tried, Laurence thinks with regret, it wouldn't be so difficult to get along.

It's annoying, thinks Laurence, I never remember my dreams. Jean-Charles has one to tell her about every morning, precise, a little baroque, the way they always are in books or films. Whereas I have nothing. Everything that happens to me in the dark folds of the night is real, a life that concerns me but eludes me. If I knew what it was about, it might help me (to do what?). She knows, at any rate, why she wakes up in the morning feeling oppressed: Dominique. Dominique – who hasn't so much carved her own path in life as hacked it out with an axe, crushing and scattering anything and anyone who bothered her – was now rendered impotent with rage. She had seen Gilbert again, *as friends*, and he did not tell her the name of the other woman. In a suspicious voice, she asked:

— Does she really exist?

— Why would he lie to you?

— He's so complicated!

Next I asked Jean-Charles:

— If you were me, would you have told her the truth?

— Surely not. It's always better not to get too involved in other people's business.

Dominique is holding out hope then. Shakily. On Sunday at Feuverolles, she stayed shut up in her bedroom claiming to have a headache, ravaged by Gilbert's absence, thinking: *He'll never come again*. On the telephone – she calls me every day – she described him in such dreadful terms that I couldn't understand why she cared for him so much: arrogant, narcissistic, sadistic, ferociously egotistical, sacrificing anyone and anything for the sake of his comfort and his little habits. Other times she lauds his intelligence, his force of will, his dazzling successes, and swears *He'll come back to me*. She can't decide what tactic to adopt, should she be sweet with him or fierce and unyielding? What will she do when the day comes – and it will come soon – that Gilbert confesses everything? Kill herself; kill him? I can't imagine. I have only ever known Dominique triumphant.

Laurence scrutinises the books Jean-Charles has recommended. (He laughed. *So you've made up your mind? That makes me so happy. You'll see that all the same we're living through a fairly extraordinary period.*) She flipped through them, she looked at their conclusions, they said the same thing as Jean-Charles and Gilbert: everything is better than it was before and everything will be better in the future. Some countries are off to a bad start; Sub-Saharan Africa, for instance; the population boom in China and the rest of Asia is worrying; however, thanks to synthetic proteins, contraception, automation and nuclear energy, we can assume that by 1990 we'll be seeing a civilisation marked by abundance and leisure. The earth will be united, perhaps even speaking – thanks to automatic translations – a universal language; men will eat when they're hungry, they will work a tiny percentage of the time, there will be no more pain or illness. Catherine will still be young, in 1990. But she wants to be reassured today about what's going on all around her. They need other books, with other points of view. Which ones? Proust can't help me. Neither can Fitzgerald. Yesterday I stood in front of the window display at a large bookshop. *Crowds and Power*, *The Colour Curtain*, *The Social Pathology of Enterprise*, *Psychoanalysis of the Sexual Functions of Women*, *America and the Americas*, *Towards a French Military Doctrine*, *A New Working Class*, *A New Class of Workers*, *The Space Adventure*, *Logic and Structure*, *Iran* . . . Where to start? I didn't go in.

Ask questions. But who to ask? Mona? She's really not a talker, she fits in the greatest amount of work in the shortest possible period. And I know what she would say. She'll describe the workers' condition which is not what it should be, on that everyone agrees, although with family benefits they almost all have a washing machine, a television and even a car. There's a housing shortage, but the situation is changing, look at all these new buildings, these worksites, with their red and yellow cranes in the Parisian sky. Everyone is concerned with social questions these days. Underneath it all, the real problem is: are we or are we not doing everything we can for there to be more comfort and justice on Earth? Mona thinks not. Jean-Charles says: *We never do* everything *we can, but just now we're doing a great deal*. In his view, people like Mona need to be a bit more patient, they're like Louise when she talks about being surprised they haven't yet landed on the Moon. Yesterday he said to me: *Obviously the human effects of high population density and automation are sometimes unfortunate. But who would want to get in the way of progress?*

Laurence picks up the most recent issues of *L'Express* and *Candide* from the magazine rack. On the whole, the news media – the dailies, the weeklies – prove Jean-Charles right. She opens them, now, without apprehension. No, nothing terrible is happening – apart from in Vietnam, but no one in France supports what the Americans are doing. She is glad to have overcome her anxiety, which condemned her to ignorance (more than a lack of time; one can always find the time). In the end, it's enough to look at things objectively. The difficulty is when you can't explain that to a child. Just now, Catherine seems calm. But if she gets upset again, I don't know that I'll be able to talk to her any better than before . . .

Crisis flares between Algeria and France. Laurence had read half the article when the doorbell rang: briskly, two times. Marthe. Laurence has asked her a million times not to turn up unannounced. But she is obeying orders from on high; she has become quite imperious since inspiration came to her from heaven.

— I'm not bothering you?

— A little. But since you're here you may as well stay a few minutes.

— Are you working?

— Yes.

— You work too much. Marthe looks at her sister perceptively. Unless something is wrong. You didn't seem very happy on Sunday.

— Of course I was.

— Come on! Your little sister knows you too well.

— You're wrong.

Laurence has no desire to confide in Marthe. And putting it all into words would make it seem more serious than it is. If she said: I'm worried about Maman, Catherine is making things difficult, Jean-Charles is in a foul mood, the affair I'm having is weighing on me, it would sound as if I had a whole heap of worries that were completely absorbing me. In reality, they're there and not there at the same time. She thinks about them all the time; she never thinks of them at all.

— Listen, says Marthe, there's something I wanted to ask you. I wanted to do it on Sunday, but you intimidate me.

— I intimidate you?

— You do – imagine that! And I know it's going to irritate you, but too bad. Catherine will be eleven soon, and I think you should send her to Sunday school so she can make her First Communion.

— What an idea! Neither Jean-Charles nor I believe in God.

— Still, you had her baptised.

— For Jean-Charles's mother. But now that she's no longer with us . . .

— You are running a great risk, depriving her of all religious education. We live in a Christian civilisation. Most children make their First Communion. She will reproach you later for having made this decision for her, without giving her the freedom to decide for herself.

— That's a good one! Giving her freedom means sending her to Sunday school.

— Yes. Because today in France, that's the normal thing to do. You're making her an exception, you're leaving her out.

— Don't say another word.

— I will say another word. I find Catherine to be sad, worried. She thinks about strange things. I've never tried to influence her, but I listen. Death, evil – it's hard for a child to take those things on board without a belief in God. If she had faith, it would help her.

— What strange things does she talk about?

— I don't remember, really. Marthe looks at her sister. You hadn't noticed anything?

— Of course I have. Catherine asks a lot of questions. I don't want to answer them with lies.

— It's a little arrogant of you to decide they're lies.

— No more than it is for you to call them truths. Laurence touches her sister's arm. Let's not fight. She's my daughter, I'll bring her up as I think best. You're always welcome to pray for her.

— I always do.

What cheek! It's true that it's not easy to bring children up secularly in a world saturated by religion. Catherine isn't drawn to all that. Louise is more interested than she is in the picturesque ceremonies. For Christmas, she will surely ask to go and see the nativities. Since they were very young Laurence has told them stories from the Bible and the Gospel as well as from Greek and Latin mythology and the life of Buddha. Beautiful tales elaborated around real events and people, she explained to them. Her father helped her with her little presentations. And Jean-Charles told them about how the universe was born, about nebulae and stars, the material from which the world is made, and the girls were spellbound. Louise became obsessed with an astronomy book, for children, with beautiful pictures. It was a long and concerted effort, well considered, which Marthe spared herself by sending her sons to the priests, and which she is suggesting she undo with a snap of her fingers. The arrogance!

— You really don't remember what Catherine said that was so striking? Laurence asked a bit later, walking her sister to the door.

— No. It was more a kind of feeling I got, beyond words, Marthe said thoughtfully.

Laurence closed the door behind her, annoyed. When she came home from school a little while ago, Catherine seemed happy. She's waiting for Brigitte so they can do their Latin homework together. What will they talk about? What do they talk about? When Laurence asks, Catherine is evasive. I don't think she doesn't trust me; it's as if we don't speak the same language. I gave her so much freedom while still treating her like a baby, I didn't try talking to her, so I think words overwhelm her, at least when I'm there. I can't find a way to connect. *Crisis flares between Algeria and France.* I should really finish reading this article.

— Bonjour, m'dame.

Brigitte hands Laurence a little bouquet of daisies.

— Thank you, that's very sweet.

— Look, I sewed up my hem.

— Ah yes. It looks much better that way.

When they met in the entrance hall of the Musée de l'Homme, Brigitte's skirt was still safety-pinned. Laurence hadn't said anything, but the little girl intercepted her gaze and her ears went red.

— Oh! I forgot again.

— Try to remember.

— I promise I'll sew it back up tonight.

Laurence took them around the museum. Louise was a bit bored; the two others ran this way and that, exclaiming. That evening, Brigitte said to Catherine:

— You're so lucky to have such a nice mother!

No special powers of divination necessary to see that her grown-up affectations hid the disorder of a young person with no one to look after them.

— Are you going to work on your Latin translations?

— Yes.

— And then you'll talk like a pair of old gossips.

Laurence hesitates.

— Brigitte, please don't tell Catherine about things that are upsetting.

Her whole face went purple, even her neck.

— What did I say that I shouldn't have?

— Nothing in particular. Laurence smiles reassuringly. It's just that Catherine is still so young, and she often cries at night; she's still scared of so many things.

— Oh! Really!

Brigitte seems more disconcerted than contrite.

— But if she asks me questions, should I tell her you've said I'm not allowed to answer?

Now Laurence is uncomfortable: I feel like I'm in the wrong for making her feel in the wrong, whereas deep down—

— What kinds of questions?

— I don't know. Things I've seen on television.

Of course! There's that, too: television. Jean-Charles has big dreams as to what it might become, but he loathes what it is currently; he hardly watches it, except for the news and *Cinq colonnes à la une* which Laurence occasionally watches as well. Sometimes what they show is unbearable, and for a child, pictures are stronger than words.

— What have you seen on television lately?

— Oh, so many things.

— Sad things?

Brigitte looks Laurence in the eyes.

— I find a lot of things sad. Don't you?

— Yes, of course.

What had been on these past few days? I should have watched. Famine in India? Mass murder in Vietnam? Race riots in America?

— I haven't watched recently, Laurence responds. What were you particularly affected by?

— Girls putting pieces of carrot on herring fillet, Brigitte says emphatically.

— What?

— Yes! They talk about how they spend the whole day putting carrot on herring fillet. They're not much older than me. I'd rather die than live that way!

— It must not be the same for them.

— Why?

— They've been brought up differently.

— They didn't seem very happy, says Brigitte.

Inane jobs, soon to be replaced by machines, but until then, obviously . . . Silence falls between them.

— Well, all right. Go ahead and do your homework. And thank you for the flowers, says Laurence.

Brigitte doesn't move.

— I can't tell Catherine about them?

— About whom?

— Those little girls.

— Of course you can. It's just when something strikes you as really horrible that it's better to keep it to yourself. I'm afraid Catherine will have nightmares.

Brigitte twists her belt around. Normally she's so direct and easy to talk to; she seems disorientated. I've gone about this all wrong, Laurence thinks; she's unhappy with herself; but how should she have gone about it? I trust your judgement, she says, awkwardly, just try to be a little more thoughtful, that's all.

Have I been insensitive or is Brigitte particularly vulnerable? she asks herself, when the door has closed. *Pieces of carrot, all day long.* No doubt if those girls do that kind of work, they're not capable of doing anything more interesting. But it must not be very nice for them. More of that *human effect,* so unfortunate. Am I right or am I wrong to care so little about it?

Laurence finishes reading the article – she doesn't like to

leave things unfinished. And then she throws herself into her work, writing a script for a brand of shampoo. She smokes cigarette after cigarette. Even stupid things can become interesting if we try to do them well. The pack is empty. It's late. A muffled sound comes from the other end of the apartment. Is Brigitte still here? And what is Louise up to? Laurence walks down the hallway. Louise is crying in her bedroom, and Catherine sounds upset, too.

— Don't cry, she's begging, I promise I don't love Brigitte more than you.

There you have it! Why does some people's pleasure always come at the expense of other people's tears!

— Loulou, you're the one I love the most. I like talking to Brigitte, but you're my little sister.

— Is that true? Really true?

Laurence tiptoes away. The tender heartbreak of childhood, when kisses are mixed with tears. It doesn't matter if Catherine isn't doing as well in school; she's maturing, she's beginning to grasp things you can't learn in class: how to empathise, console, give and take, how to read in someone's face or hear in their voice nuances that escape her. For a moment, Laurence's heart warms: a precious, rare heat. What wouldn't she do, so that Catherine should never find herself deprived of it later on?

3

Laurence takes advantage of the children's absence to tidy up their rooms. Maybe Brigitte didn't tell her about the television show that made such an impression on her; in any case Catherine didn't seem upset at all. She was overjoyed this morning when she and Louise were placed in their grandfather's car: he was taking them away to the Loire Valley for the weekend, to see the châteaux. Laurence was the one who – pretty stupidly it must be said – let herself be bothered by what she'd heard. The idea of a drab and daily misfortune seemed more difficult to digest than a great catastrophe, however unusual. She wanted to know how other people dealt with it.

She interrogated Lucien about it at lunch on Monday. (These meetings are so disagreeable. He's angry with me, but he's hooked. Dominique, ten years ago: *Men, I'm sick to the teeth of them*. Get there late, cancel, agree with them less and less: they lose interest in the end. I don't know how to do it.

One of these days I'm going to have to make my mind up to leave him, and it's going to be bloody.) He's barely interested in these problems, but he responded anyway. A sixteen-year-old girl, condemned to an idiotic job, barred from having a future, it's terrible, yes; but life is always terrible, if not for one reason then for another. I have a little money, I make a lot, and what good does it do me, if you don't love me? Who's happy? Do you know anyone who's happy? You avoid real heartbreak by closing off your heart – I don't call that happy. Your husband? Maybe, but if he learned the truth he would not be pleased. All life is valuable, more or less. You said it yourself: it's pathetic what motivates people, their stupid fantasies, their illusions. They have nothing solid to hold on to, nothing that's really important to them; they wouldn't buy so many tranquillisers or anti-anxiety pills if they were happy. There is the unhappiness of the poor, but also of the rich. You should read Fitzgerald, he writes about it incredibly well. Yes, thinks Laurence, there's truth in what he says. Jean-Charles is often cheerful, but not really happy; he is too quick to anger, whether it's one thing or another he's set off too easily. Maman, with her beautiful apartment, her clothes, her country house, what hell awaits her! And me? I don't know. I seem to be missing something other people have. Unless – unless they don't have it either. Maybe when Gisèle Dufrène sighs *It's marvellous*, when a luminous smile spreads across Marthe's enormous mouth, they don't feel any more than I do. Only Papa . . .

Laurence had him all to herself last Wednesday, after the girls went to sleep; Jean-Charles was having dinner out with some young architects. (*No more verticals, no more horizontals, architecture will be oblique or it won't be at all.* He found it a little farcical but they still had some interesting perspectives, he told her when he got home.) Once again she tried to put order to what he had told her, jumping from one thing to the next. Whatever the country, socialist or capitalist, man is crushed by technology, alienated from his labour, shackled and chained, dehumanised. All of this stems from the fact that he increased his needs when he should have been content to satisfy the ones he had; instead of trying to create an abundance that doesn't and may well never exist, he should have been happy with the essentials, as is the case in some impoverished communities – in Sardinia or in Greece, for example – as yet unreached by industry, uncorrupted by money. In these places people are austerely happy because they have preserved certain values, truly human values like dignity, fraternity, generosity, which gives their lives their unique character. As long as we continue to invent new requirements, we will continue to increase our frustrations. When did this decline begin? The day when we chose science over wisdom, practicality over beauty. With the Renaissance, rationalism, capitalism, positivism. All right. But now that it's happened, what can we do? Try to revive wisdom and an appreciation of beauty within oneself and in others. Only a moral revolution – not a social or a political or an industrial revolution – will restore man's lost truth to him. At least we can carry out this transformation in our own lives – so we insist on joy, in spite of the absurdity and the mess that surrounds us.

The things Papa tells her sound a lot like what she hears from Lucien. Everyone is unhappy; everyone can find happiness. One thing amounted to the other. Can I explain to Catherine that people are not as miserable as all that, because they still fight to be alive? Laurence hesitates. It would be like saying that unhappy people aren't actually unhappy. Is it true? What about Dominique, her voice broken with sobbing and shouting – she's horrified by her life, but she doesn't want to die. That's unhappiness. And then there is that emptiness, that void, which chills her blood, which is worse than death, even if we prefer it to death because we don't actually kill ourselves – I encountered it five years ago, and an atrocious memory of it stays with me. And the fact is that people kill themselves – he asked for bananas and a napkin – because there is something worse than death. It's the coldness in the bones when you read about someone's suicide – not the frail corpse hanging from the bars of the window, but what happened in his heart just before he did it.

No, to think about it carefully, Laurence thinks, what Papa told me is really only true for him; he's always borne everything with such stoicism, his renal colic and his operation, his four years in the stalag, being left by Maman, even though he felt deeply sad. And he alone is capable of finding joy in the cloistered, austere life he's chosen for himself. I would like to know what his secret is. Maybe if I saw him more often, spent more time with him . . .

— Are you ready? Jean-Charles asks. They go down to the garage, and Jean-Charles opens the door.

— Let me drive, says Laurence. You're too irritable.

He smiles good-naturedly.

— As you like. And he sits in the car beside her. His conversation with Vergne must have been very disagreeable; he didn't talk about it, but he's been in a foul mood, he's been driving dangerously, much too fast, suddenly hitting the brakes and yelling. For a while yesterday the local papers might have had another fracas between drivers to write about.

The other day at the office, Lucien gave a brilliant disquisition on the psychology of a male driver: frustration, compensation, power and isolation. (He himself drives very well, but incredibly fast.) Mona interrupted him:

— I'm going to tell you why all these very polite men become brutes when they're behind the wheel.

— Why?

— Because they're brutes.

Lucien shrugged. What was she getting at?

— Monday, when we get back, I'm signing with Monnod, Jean-Charles said in a cheerful voice.

— Are you happy?

— Ridiculously. I'm going to spend Sunday sleeping and

playing badminton. And Monday I'll start off on the right foot.

The car emerges from the tunnel. Laurence speeds up, her eyes on the rear-view mirror. Overtake, fall behind, overtake, overtake, fall behind. Saturday night: Paris has just finished emptying out. She likes to drive and Jean-Charles doesn't have the annoying habit most husbands do – no matter what he thinks about her driving, he keeps his comments to himself. She smiles. He doesn't have very many faults, overall, and when they drive, side by side, she often has the illusion – though she doesn't like the cliché – that they are *made for each other.* She thinks decisively: this week I'm going to have a talk with Lucien. He said it to her again yesterday: you don't love anyone! Is it true? No, of course not. I love him. I'm going to leave him, but I love him. I love everyone. Except Gilbert.

She exits the autoroute and drives along a small, deserted road. Gilbert will be at Feuverolles. Dominique was triumphant on the phone. *Gilbert will be there.* Why is he coming? Maybe he's playing the friendship card – he won't be much further ahead the day the truth comes out. Or was he coming over to tell her everything? Laurence's hands are damp on the wheel. Dominique has survived the past month because she hasn't given up hope.

— I wonder why Gilbert agreed to come.

— Maybe he's given up his plans to get married.

— I doubt it.

It is cold and grey outside, the flowers have died, but the windows shine in the night, and a big fire is burning in the living room. The few people that are there are first rate, inner circle: the Dufrènes, Gilbert, Thirion and his wife. Laurence knew him when she was a little girl, he worked with her father; now he's become the most famous lawyer in France. This is why Marthe and Hubert haven't been invited – they don't come off well. Smiles, handshakes; Gilbert kisses the hand Laurence had refused him a month ago. His gaze is heavy with implied meaning when he asks her:

— Would you like something to drink?

— Later, says Dominique. She takes Laurence by the shoulder. First let's go upstairs and fix your hair, you've completely come undone. In the bedroom she smiles. You haven't come undone at all, I just wanted to speak with you.

— What's wrong?

— Such pessimism!

Dominique's eyes are shining. She's a little too elegant with her *belle époque* blouse and her long skirt (who is she imitating?). She says in an excited voice:

— Would you believe it? I've finally uncovered the truth.

— Really?

If Dominique knows the truth, then why the mischievous behaviour?

— Get ready, you're going to be very surprised. She takes her time. Gilbert has gone back to one of his old loves: Lucile de Saint-Chamont.

— What makes you think that's the case?

— I've been well informed. He spends all his time holed up at her place. Every weekend he's at the Manoir. Funny, isn't it? After all the things he's told me about her! I wonder how she did it. She's cleverer than I thought.

Laurence keeps quiet. She hates this feeling of superiority – it's so unjust – of knowing something someone else doesn't. Should she tell her what she knows? Not today, with all these people in the house.

— Maybe it's not Lucile, maybe it's one of her friends.

— Come on! She wouldn't encourage Gilbert to have an affair with another woman. I understand why he wouldn't tell me her name: he was afraid I'd laugh in his face. I can't quite understand this caprice of his, but in any case it can't possibly last. Gilbert dropped her the moment he met me, he must have had his reasons – and they can't have changed. He'll come back to me.

Laurence says nothing. The silence wears on. Dominique should find that surprising, but no, she's so accustomed to asking all the questions and providing all the answers. She goes on, in a dreamy voice:

— It might be worth sending Lucile a little note detailing his anatomy, and his preferences.

Laurence starts.

— You can't do that!

— It would be hilarious. Imagine her face! His face! No. He'd hate me for life. My tactic, on the other hand, is to be very, very sweet. Win back some of my previous position. I'm hoping much will come from our trip to Baalbek.

— You think the trip is still happening?

— What? Of course it is! Dominique's voice gets higher. He promised me for months that we'd spend Christmas there. Everyone knows about it. He can't back out now.

— But the other woman will say he can't go.

— I will simply give him an ultimatum: if he doesn't come with me, I'll never see him again.

— He won't give in to blackmail.

— He won't want to lose me. This thing with Lucile isn't serious.

— So why did he tell you about it?

— Sadism, I'm sure, in part. And then he needed to free up his weekends. But you see – all I had to do was insist a little bit, and he came.

— Well, then, give him the ultimatum.

Maybe that was the solution. Dominique will be able to tell herself that she's the one who left him. And later, when she learns the truth, the hard part will be behind her.

People are laughing and talking loudly in the living room, drinking wine, bourbon, martinis. Jean-Charles hands Laurence a glass of pineapple juice.

— Nothing too bad?

— No. Nothing good either. Look at her.

Dominique is resting a possessive hand on Gilbert's shoulder.

— When I think you haven't been here in three weeks! You work too hard. It's important to be able to relax.

— I know very well, he says in a neutral voice.

— No, she says, there's nothing like the countryside to help you truly relax.

She smiles at him flirtatiously, impishly; it doesn't suit her at all. Her voice is too loud.

— Or travel, she adds. Her hand still grasping Gilbert's arm, she tells Thirion: We're going to spend Christmas in Baalbek.

— Excellent idea. They say it's magnificent.

— Yes. And I'm eager to see what Christmas is like in a hot country. We always picture Christmas in the snow . . .

Gilbert doesn't respond. Dominique is so tense that she'd explode at the slightest word. He must feel it.

— Our friend Luzarches had a charming idea, says Mme Thirion in her blonde, sing-song voice. A surprise New Year's Eve in an aeroplane. He boarded twenty-five of us, and we didn't know if we were going to London, to Rome, to Amsterdam, or somewhere else entirely. And of course he'd reserved enough tables for us all at the loveliest restaurant in town.

— How amusing, says Dominique.

— People usually have such limited imaginations when it comes to amusing themselves, says Gilbert.

Another one of those words that has lost its meaning for Laurence. Sometimes she finds a film interesting, or it makes her laugh, but did it amuse her? Does Gilbert amuse himself? Taking an aeroplane without knowing where it's heading – is that amusing? That suspicion she'd had the other day – perhaps it was justified.

She goes to sit with Jean-Charles and the Dufrènes near the fire.

— It's too bad that in our modern buildings we can't enjoy the luxury of a fireplace, says Jean-Charles.

He looks into the flames; the firelight dances on his face. He's taken off his suede jacket, and opened the collar of his checked Western shirt; he seems younger, more relaxed than usual. (Dufrène as well, in his corduroy suit; is it just a question of what they're wearing?)

— I forgot to tell you something your father will love to hear. Goldwater loves woodfires so much that in the summer he air-conditions his house till it's freezing and then lights huge blazes everywhere.

Laurence laughs.

— Oh yes, Papa will love that.

On a side table nearby, there are some magazines – *Réalité*, *L'Express*, *Candide*, *Votre Jardin* – and a few books, whatever's won the Goncourt or the Renaudot. Records are scattered on the divan, although Dominique never listens to music. Laurence looks at her again. She is smiling, relaxed, she gesticulates a great deal when she talks.

— Well! I prefer to have dinner at Maxim's. At least I can be sure the chef hasn't spat on the plates and I won't be squished in beside the man at the next table. I know, everyone's terribly snobby about little bistros these days, but it ends up being just as expensive, it smells of grease, and you can't so much as move a finger without bumping into someone else.

— Have you not been to Chez Gertrude?

— Of course. For that price I prefer La Tour d'Argent.

She seems completely at ease. Why did Gilbert come? Laurence hears Jean-Charles laugh, and then the Dufrènes.

— No but seriously, between the builders, the developers, the managers, the engineers, we poor architects are getting completely lost! says Jean-Charles.

— Ah! the developers, sighs Dufrène.

Jean-Charles pokes at the fire, his eyes shining. Were there woodfires in his childhood? In any case there is such an air of innocence on his face that Laurence feels something melt in her, such tenderness. If only she could get it back for good, for always . . . Dominique's voice breaks her from her reverie.

— I also thought it wouldn't be very amusing, and it certainly got off to a bad start; their system had completely broken down, we had to stand for an hour before they let us in, but in any case it was worth it, anyone who is anyone was there. The champagne was acceptable. And I have to say, I found Mme de Gaulle far superior to what I expected, not very stylish, no, she's no Linette Verdelet, but she is very dignified.

— I've heard only people in finance or politics are allowed to eat; people who work in the arts or in publishing are only allowed to drink, is that true? Gilbert asks in a nonchalant voice.

— We didn't go there to eat, Dominique says with a dry little laugh.

What a bastard Gilbert is, asking that question with the express purpose of being disagreeable! Dufrène turns towards him:

— Is it true they're thinking of using IBM machines to create abstract paintings?

— They might be. But I can't imagine it would make anyone any money, says Gilbert, smiling roundly.

— What! How could a machine paint! exclaims Mme Thirion.

— Abstract – why not? says Thirion, ironic.

— Did you know that some of them can produce music that sounds like Mozart or Bach? says Dufrène. But here's the catch: their works are perfect, whereas music written by flesh-and-blood musicians is always flawed in some way.

Oh! I read that somewhere recently, in one of the weekly magazines. Since she's started paying attention to the news Laurence has noticed that conversations often reproduce things other people have written in articles. Why not? They have to get their information from somewhere.

— Soon the machines will replace our studios and we'll be out on our ears, says Jean-Charles.

— Most definitely, says Gilbert. We are entering a new phase, in which men are becoming useless.

— Not us! says Thirion. There will always be a need for lawyers, because a machine will never be capable of eloquence.

— But maybe people won't care about eloquence any more, says Jean-Charles.

— Come on! Man is a linguistic animal, and he will always be seduced by language. Machines will not change human nature.

— That's just it – they absolutely will!

Jean-Charles and Dufrène agree with each other (they have read the same articles), the whole idea of mankind is at stake, and will no doubt disappear; it's a nineteenth-century invention, it's outdated. In every field – literature, music, painting, architecture – art rejects the previous generations with their humanism. Gilbert sits quietly, indulgently, as the others speak over each other. OK, there are books that can no longer be written, films we can no longer see, music we can no longer listen to, but a masterpiece, that's timeless! What is a masterpiece anyway? Subjective criteria must be eliminated, it's impossible, sorry, but that's what all the modern critics try to do, and what about the criteria for the Goncourts and the Renaudots, I'd like to know what those are, every year the winners are worse and worse, ah! but that's the editors' fault, what a racket, I have it on authority that certain of the judges have been bought, that's shameful, for the painters it's even worse, any old dabbler can become a genius with a little good publicity, if people say he's a genius he's a genius, what a paradox, no, there are no other criteria, no objective criteria.

— Oh but still! What is beautiful is beautiful! says Mme Thirion with such passion that for a moment everyone falls silent.

Then they're back at it again.

As usual, Laurence is lost in her own thoughts; she almost always disagrees with whatever is being said, but since they never agree amongst themselves, by contradicting them she ends up contradicting herself. Although Mme Thirion is a certifiable idiot, I am tempted to agree with her: what is beautiful is beautiful; what is true is true. But what is such an opinion worth? Where does it come from? From Papa, from lycée, from Mlle Houchet. When I was eighteen, I had convictions. Something of them remains, not much, more a kind of nostalgia. She doubts her own judgement: it's such a question of mood and circumstance. I'm hardly capable, when I leave the cinema, of saying whether or not I liked the film.

— May I speak with you a moment?

Laurence stares coldly at Gilbert.

— I haven't the least desire to.

— I insist.

Laurence follows him into the next room, out of curiosity, out of concern. They sit; she waits.

— I wanted to warn you that I'm going to break the news to Dominique. This trip is obviously out of the question. And Patricia has been very sympathetic, very human, but she believes she's waited long enough. We are going to be married in late May.

Gilbert has made up his mind. The only solution is to murder him – Dominique would suffer much less. She murmurs:

— Why did you come? You've given her false hope.

— I came for several reasons. I don't want to make an enemy of Dominique, and she really put our friendship on the line. If I can make a few concessions here and there in order to smooth out the break-up, that's certainly to be preferred, especially for her sake, don't you agree?

— You can't.

— Yes, I can, he says in a different voice. I also came to see how she was taking things. She persists in believing this is a passing fancy. I have to open her eyes.

— Not now!

— I'm going back to Paris tonight.

Gilbert's face lit up:

— Listen. What I'm wondering is if it wouldn't be better for you to try to prepare her for it. If it wouldn't be better for her.

— Ah, that's your real reason for coming. You want me to do your dirty work.

— I will admit that I do detest a scene.

— Because you lack imagination. There are worse things than a scene. Laurence thinks for a moment.

— Do something for me. Refuse to go on the trip, without talking to Patricia about it. Dominique will be so angry she'll break up with you herself.

— You know very well that won't work, Gilbert says dismissively.

He's right. Laurence wanted to believe, for a moment, in what Dominique had said – *I'll give him an ultimatum* – but no matter the tears and reproaches she'll continue to wait, to demand, to hope.

— What you're going to do is horrible.

— Your hostility pains me, says Gilbert, sounding wounded. No man is master of his own heart. I no longer love Dominique, I love Patricia. What crime have I committed?

The word *love* in his mouth sounds obscene.

— I will speak to her this week. And I would ask that you go and see her soon afterwards.

Laurence looks at him with hatred:

— To prevent her from doing herself in, leaving a note explaining why? It would be terrible to have her blood staining Patricia's white dress . . .

She stalks off. Lobsters screech in her ears, a terrible sound of inhuman suffering. She goes to the buffet and pours herself a glass of champagne. They refill their plates while they carry on the conversation they've begun.

— This girl has talent, says Mme Thirion, but someone

has to teach her how to dress herself, she's perfectly capable of wearing a polka-dot blouse with a striped skirt.

— That doesn't sound so terrible, says Gisèle Dufrène.

— If you have a genius for a dressmaker you can wear whatever you like, says Dominique.

She draws close to Laurence.

— What did Gilbert say?

— Oh! He wanted to tell me about the niece of one of his friends who's interested in advertising.

— Are you lying?

— You can't possibly think Gilbert would talk to me about his relationship with you?

— With him anything is possible. You're not eating?

Laurence has lost her appetite. She sinks into an armchair and picks up a magazine. She feels incapable of engaging in any conversation. He'll talk to her during the week. Who will help me to calm Dominique? It struck Laurence during her mother's month-long solitude: so many acquaintances, and not a single friend. No one to listen to her, or simply to distract her. What fragile constructions our lives are, which no one can bolster but ourselves. Is it this way for everyone? Still, I have Papa. And Jean-Charles, for that matter, who would never make me unhappy. She lifts her eyes to him. He talks, he laughs, people laugh around him, he is very charming when he makes an effort. Again a surge of tenderness goes through Laurence. It's normal, after all, for him to have been a bit agitated these past few days. He knows what he owes Vergne, but all the same he can't sacrifice all his ambitions for him. He was so torn about it, that's why he was in such a bad mood. He wants to succeed, and Laurence understands. Work would be terribly boring if we didn't get a little competitive from time to time.

— My dear Dominique, I'm so sorry, but I really must be going, says Gilbert ceremoniously.

— Already?

— I came early because I had to leave early, he says.

He does the rounds, saying goodbye quickly. Dominique leaves the house with him. Jean-Charles signals to Laurence.

— Come here! Thirion is telling us fascinating stories about his trials.

They're all sitting down, except for Thirion who is pacing back and forth, twitching an imaginary lawyer's gown.

— What do I think of my female colleagues, dear madam? he asks Gisèle. The utmost good. Many of them are charming women and many of them have talent (these are not often the same women). But one thing is sure: none of them will ever be able to plead a case in criminal court. They don't have the lungs for it! Or the authority. Or – this will surprise you – the necessary sense of drama.

— We've seen plenty of women succeed in careers that seemed closed to them at the outset, says Jean-Charles.

— I swear to you – the cleverest of women, the most eloquent: in front of a jury I would swallow her whole.

— You may yet be surprised, says Jean-Charles. Personally I think the future belongs to women.

— Maybe, but on the condition that they don't just mimic the men.

— Doing a man's job doesn't mean mimicking the men.

— Oh, Jean-Charles, says Gisèle Dufrène, you're always so fashionable, don't tell me you're a feminist. Feminism is so passé.

Feminism: it seems everyone is talking about it, these days. Laurence immediately tunes out. It's like psychoanalysis, the common market, nuclear deterrents, she doesn't know what to think, she doesn't think anything at all. I'm allergic to thinking. She watches her mother who's come back into the room with a tight smile on her lips. Tomorrow, the day after tomorrow, this week, Gilbert will tell her everything. In the relaxation corner her voice had echoed – *Bastard! The bastard!* – and it will once again. Again Laurence can see the flowers like aggressive birds. When she returns to herself, Mme Thirion is saying vehemently:

— The incessant disparagement makes me sick. It really is a good idea: at the benefit on the twenty-fifth for the starving children, for twenty thousand francs they're serving what the little Indian children eat: a bowl of rice and a glass of water. And the left-wing press won't stop sniggering! What would they say if we ate caviar and foie gras!

— We can always find something to criticise if we try, says Dominique. You just have to let it go.

She appears absent-minded, seems distracted when she replies to Mme Thirion, while the others gather round a bridge table; Laurence opens *L'Express*. Broken up into little columns, the news goes down like a glass of milk. She's sleepy. She gets up eagerly when Thirion leaves the bridge table, announcing:

— I have a busy day tomorrow. We must be going.

— I'm going to go up to bed, she says.

— I always sleep so well here. No sedatives necessary. In Paris I can't do without them.

— I've cut back on the sleeping pills since I've started taking a harmoniser every day, says Gisèle Dufrène.

— I tried one of those lullaby records, but I wasn't lulled, says Jean-Charles, with a twinkle.

— I've heard about an astonishing device, says Thirion: you turn it on, and it produces these fascinating, monotonous flashes of light, and it sends you straight to sleep. Then it turns itself off! I'm going to order one.

— Well, I don't need any of that tonight, says Laurence.

These rooms really are splendid, walls upholstered in toile de Jouy, with rustic wooden beds, patchwork quilts, a faience jug and bowl on the washstand. An almost invisible door in the wall leads to the bathroom. She leans out the window and breathes in the cold smell of earth. In a moment Jean-Charles will be there – she doesn't want to think of him any more, his profile illuminated by the dancing light of the flames. And suddenly he's there, he takes her in his arms, and the tenderness she felt before becomes a burning rush of desire through her veins, she is knocked backwards with the force of it, and their lips meet.

— You poor thing! You must have been so afraid.

   — No, says Laurence. I was just glad I didn't hit that cyclist.

She leans her head back against the comfortable leather armchair. She's vaguely unhappy, without knowing why.

— Would you like a cup of tea?

— Oh, don't go to any trouble.

— It'll take me five minutes.

Badminton on the television. It was dark when we left, I wasn't driving very fast. I felt Jean-Charles's presence beside me, I remembered the night we'd had, while scanning the road ahead. Suddenly a cyclist appeared in my headlights, a redhead, from somewhere on my right. I yanked the wheel, the car pitched to the left, and rolled over into the ditch.

— Are you OK?

— I'm OK. Are you OK?

— I'm OK.

He turned off the engine. The door opened.

— Are you hurt?

— No.

A group of cyclists, young men and women, surrounded

the car, which was upside down in the ditch, its wheels spinning. I yelled at the redhead *You idiot!* But what a relief! I thought I'd driven over his body. I flung myself into Jean-Charles's arms.

— My love! What a lucky escape. Not a single scratch on either of us!

He wasn't smiling.

— The car is wrecked.

— That's true. But better it than us.

Some other drivers stopped, and one of the young men explained:

— This idiot wasn't looking where he was going, he nearly cycled into the car, so this nice woman had to swerve to the left.

The redhead was stammering out his apologies, the others were thanking me.

— That was a lucky escape! He really owes you one.

By the side of this soggy road, next to the wreck of our car, a feeling of joy rose in me, heady as champagne. I loved this idiot cyclist because I hadn't killed him, and his friends who were smiling at me, and these strangers who offered to drive us to Paris. And suddenly my head was spinning and I passed out.

She had regained consciousness in the back of a Citroën DS. But she had trouble remembering the drive back – she had indeed suffered a great shock. Jean-Charles was saying that they'd have to buy a new car and that you can't just pull two hundred thousand francs out of nowhere; he was understandably unhappy; but what Laurence had trouble accepting was that he seemed to be angry with her. It really wasn't my fault, I'm actually rather proud of how gently I landed us in the ditch, but nevertheless, all husbands have themselves convinced that they're better drivers than their wives. Yes, I remember now, he was so unfair last night when we were going to bed, I said:

— If I hadn't wrecked the car we all would have been very badly hurt.

And he responded:

— I don't think it was a very clever thing to do, we only have third-party insurance.

— You'd rather I'd killed the guy?

— You wouldn't have killed him. Maybe just broken a leg.

— I could very well have killed him.

— Well, it would have served him right. Everyone would have testified in your favour.

He says that without really thinking, just to be disagreeable, because he's convinced I should have been able to manage it in a less expensive way. Well, he's wrong.

— Here's the tea, my special blend, says her father, placing the tray on the table piled high with magazines. You know what I'm wondering, he says. If the girls had been in the car, would you have had the same reaction?

— I don't know, says Laurence. She hesitates. Jean-Charles is an extension of myself. We're a team – I acted as if I were alone. But to endanger my daughters to save a stranger would have been absurd! And what about Jean-Charles? Given where he was sitting, he could have been very badly hurt, he could even have been killed. He does have some right to be angry.

Her father responds:

— Yesterday, with the children, I would have run over a pensioner rather than take even the smallest risk.

— How happy they were! says Laurence. You treated them like queens.

— Ah! I took them to one of those little inns where you can still get real cream, chicken fed with good grains, real eggs. Did you know that in America they feed their hens sea-weed and inject the eggs with chemicals to make them taste more like eggs?

— That doesn't surprise me. Dominique brought me chocolate from New York that was chemically flavoured to taste like chocolate.

They laugh together. To think that I've never spent a weekend with him! He serves the tea in mismatched mugs. A light bulb in an old gas lamp lights the table, where a volume of the Pléiade is open – he has the complete collection. He doesn't have any trouble amusing himself.

— Louise is incredibly bright, he says. But Catherine is more like you. You had the same seriousness, at her age.

— Yes, I was a lot like her, says Laurence. (Will she be a lot like me?)

— I think her imagination has developed a great deal.

— I know! And Marthe wants me to take her to get her First Communion!

— She wants to convert us all. She doesn't preach, she just offers herself as an example. As if to say: look at how faith can transform a woman, look how beautiful she can become on the inside. But – poor thing, in her case transposing that beauty to the outside isn't easy.

— You're so mean!

— Oh, she's a good girl. You and your mother have successful careers, but being a housewife is so drab. So she's gone all in on sainthood.

— And having Hubert as the only witness to her life is obviously not enough.

— Who was at Feuverolles?

— Gilbert Mortier, the Dufrènes, Thirion and his wife.

— She allows that toad into her house! You remember when he came over – he was forever holding forth, with nothing actually to say. Without wanting to brag, I had a better start than he did. His whole career is based on dirty tricks and good publicity. And that's what Dominique wanted me to become!

— You couldn't have.

— I could have if I had done the disgusting things he did.

— That's what I mean.

Dominique refused to understand. *He chose mediocrity.* No. He chose not to compromise, to have the time to reflect and cultivate his interests, instead of the frenetic lifestyle everyone leads in Maman's circle, that I lead, too.

— Is your mother still thriving?

Laurence hesitates.

— It's not going so well with Gilbert Mortier. I think he's going to leave her.

— That must have been a shock! She's more intelligent than Miss World and better to look at than Mrs Roosevelt – so she thinks she's superior to all other women.

— For the moment she's very unhappy.

Laurence understands why her father is so harsh, but she pities Dominique.

— You know, I thought about what you told me, about misfortune. It does exist, you know. You are in control of every situation, but that's just not possible for everyone.

— What I do, everyone can do. I'm not exceptional.

— I think you are, says Laurence with tenderness. For example: living alone. Very few people would be able to stand it.

— Because they don't really try. My greatest joys have come in moments of solitude.

— Are you really happy with your life?

— I don't regret any of my choices.

— You're lucky.

— You're not happy with yours?

— Of course I am! But there are things I regret. I don't take care of my daughters enough; I see too little of them.

— You have your house and your job.

— Yes, but still . . .

Without Lucien I would have more time to myself, she thinks; I would see Papa more, and I could be like him, reading, reflecting. My life is overstuffed with things.

— You see, now I have to get going. She stands up. Your special blend was delicious.

— Tell me though, are you sure you don't have any internal bleeding? You should see a doctor.

— No, no. I'm perfectly fine.

— What are you going to do without a car? Do you want to borrow mine?

— I couldn't deprive you of it.

— It wouldn't deprive me, I use it so rarely. I would much rather wander about on foot.

So typical of him, she thinks, getting behind the wheel. He's nobody's fool, and his tongue can turn sharp, but he's so present, so attentive, always ready to lend a hand. She feels herself surrounded, still, by the warm half-light of the apartment. Unburden my life. I have to let Lucien go.

Tonight's the night, she decides. She said she was going out with Mona, and Jean-Charles believed her, he still believes her, he lacks imagination. He is certainly not cheating on her and jealousy doesn't interest him.

— It's pretty here, don't you think?

— Very pretty, she says.

After an hour at Lucien's she insisted they go out. It seemed easier to explain herself in a public place than in the privacy of his bedroom. He took her to an elegant *belle époque* cabaret: soft lighting, mirrors, green plants, discreet niches with sofas. She could have dreamed up a place like this for a champagne commercial, or some aged cognac. One of the pitfalls of the job – she knows only too well how to set a scene like this; they always come apart as she looks at them.

— What will you have? They've got a remarkable whisky collection.

— Order me one, and you can drink it.

— You look beautiful tonight.

She smiles, kindly:

— You always say that.

— I always mean it.

In the mirror she looks herself over. A pretty woman, discreetly happy, somewhat mysterious and given to whims, that's how Lucien sees me. That pleases me. For Jean-Charles she is efficient, loyal, lucid. He's wrong, too. Nice to look at, all right. But plenty of women are better-looking. A brunette with pearly white skin and big green eyes set off by tremendously thick false eyelashes is dancing with a boy a bit younger than she is. I can understand why a man would lose his heart to such a creature. They smile at each other, and from time to time their cheeks touch. Is that love? We also smile at each other, and our hands touch.

— If you only knew how hard the weekends are! Saturday night – the other nights I still have my doubts. But Saturday night I know for certain. It's a flaming red pit at the end of my week. I got drunk.

— You shouldn't have. It doesn't matter that much.

— I don't matter that much, either.

She doesn't answer. How dull he's become! Always reproaching me for something. If he does it one more time, I'll take that as my cue: *While we're on the subject . . .*

— Do you want to dance? he asks.

— Let's dance.

Tonight's the night, she repeats to herself. Why, though? Not because of that night at Feuverolles, it doesn't bother her to go from one bed to another; they're so very much the same. And Jean-Charles chilled her to the bone when she threw herself into his arms after the accident and he just replied, so uncaringly, *The car is totally wrecked*. The real reason, the only reason, is that love is tedious if you're no longer in it. All that wasted time. They fall into silence, as they so often do, but can he feel that it's no longer the same silence?

Well now, how to begin, she wonders, as she sits back down on the sofa. She lights a cigarette. In all the old-fashioned novels they're forever lighting cigarettes, it's so artificial, says Jean-Charles. But we often do it in real life when we need to look composed.

— You're not lighting your cigarette with a cheap little lighter? he says. You're usually more tasteful than that! It's so ugly.

— It's practical.

— I would so like to give you a really beautiful one. Really beautiful. Made of gold. But I'm not allowed to give you presents.

— Come on! That's never stopped you.

— Cheap rubbish.

Perfumes, scarves, she'd said they were PR samples. But obviously Jean-Charles would notice a gold powder compact or lighter.

— You know, I don't much care about *things*. Working in publicity, selling them all the time, I've really gone off them.

— I don't see the relationship. A beautiful object is made to last, it's full of memories. This lighter, for instance, I used it to light your cigarettes the first time you came over.

— We don't need a lighter to remember that.

Essentially — though in a different way to Jean-Charles — Lucien also lives outside of himself. Papa is the only one I know who doesn't. His loyalties are within his being, not in the things he owns.

— Why are you being like this? asks Lucien. You wanted to go out, we went out; I'm doing what you want. You could be nicer to me.

She doesn't answer.

— All evening you've not had a tender word for me.

— There was no occasion for one.

— There never is.

Now's the time, she tells herself. He'll suffer a little, and then he'll console himself. Right this moment, dozens of other couples are breaking up; in a year he won't even think about it any more.

— Listen, she says, you're always criticising me. I think it would be better if we could be honest with each other.

— I have nothing to explain to you, he says in a lively voice. And I'm not asking anything of you.

— But you do, indirectly. And I want to respond to you. I have the deepest affection for you, I always will. But I'm no longer in love with you. (Was I ever? Do these words even mean anything?)

Silence. Laurence's heart speeds up, but the hard part is over. The definitive words have been pronounced. Now the scene must be brought to its conclusion.

— I've known that for a long time, says Lucien. Why do you feel the need to tell me tonight?

— Because we have to accept the consequences. If it's no longer love, it's better to stop sleeping together.

— But I love you. And there are plenty of people who sleep together without being madly in love.

— I don't see a reason why we should.

— Of course you don't! You have everything you need at home. Whereas I, I who can't live without you, I'm the least of your worries.

— On the contrary, you're the one I'm worried about. I give you too little, just crumbs, like you said. Another woman would make you happier.

— So thoughtful of you – I'm touched!

Lucien's face falls. He takes Laurence's hand.

— You can't be serious! Everything we've been through together, the nights in Le Havre, in my bedroom, our trip to Bordeaux – you want to erase all of that?

— Of course not. I'll always remember it.

— You've already forgotten.

He's invoking the past, he's fighting with himself; she answers each of his questions calmly; there's no point in it, but she knows what we owe someone when we break up with them; she will listen to him courteously until he's finished, it's the least she can do. He looks at her suspiciously.

— I understand! You've met someone else!

— What! With the life I lead!

— No, you're right, I don't believe it. You never loved me. You don't love anyone. There are women who are frigid in bed, but you're worse. You're frigid in the heart.

— If I am it's not my fault.

— What if I said I would go and splatter myself across the autoroute?

— You're not stupid enough to do that. Come on, let's not get overdramatic. One more or less – people really are fundamentally interchangeable, you know.

— That's a terrible thing to say. Lucien gets up. Let's go home. You're making me want to hit you.

They drive in silence until they reach Laurence's house. She gets out and stands for a moment, hesitating on the pavement.

— Well, goodbye, she says.

— No, not goodbye. Take your kindness and shove it up your arse. I'm going to move to a different company and you'll never see me again.

He closes the door and turns on the engine. She feels a twinge of shame, but also of pride. *It had to be done*, she thinks. She doesn't really know why.

She ran into Lucien today at Publinf, and they didn't speak to each other. It's ten o'clock at night. She's tidying their bedroom when she hears the phone ring, and Jean-Charles's voice saying:

— Laurence! Your mother wants to speak to you.

She goes running.

— Is that you, Dominique?

— Yes. Come straight away.

— What's wrong?

— I'll tell you when you get here.

— I'm coming.

Jean-Charles picks up his book, and asks, with an air of annoyance:

— What's going on?

— I guess Gilbert spoke to her.

— Non-stop drama!

Laurence slips on her coat and goes to kiss her daughters.

— Why are you going out now?

— Mammie isn't feeling well. She's asked me to bring her some medicine.

The lift takes her down to the garage where she parked her father's car. Gilbert's told her! She reverses, pulls out. Calm, stay calm. Breathe deeply a few times. Stay cool. Don't drive too quickly. In a stroke of luck she finds a space right away, and parks beside the kerb. She pauses for a moment, immobilised at the bottom of the stairs. She lacks the courage to climb them, to ring the bell. What will she find behind the door? She climbs, she rings.

— What's going on?

Dominique doesn't answer. Her hair and make-up are flawless, her eyes are dry; she smokes nervously.

— Gilbert's just left, she says in a dull voice. She takes Laurence into the living room. He's a bastard. The king of the bastards. His girlfriend too. All of them. But I know how to defend myself. They want to strip me of everything I have. I won't let them.

Laurence looks at her questioningly, and waits. Dominique has trouble pronouncing the next words.

— It's not Lucile. It's Patricia. That halfwit. He wants to marry her.

— To marry her?

— To marry her. Can you believe it? I can just see it. A big marriage at the Manoir, with orange flowers. At the church, because with Marie-Claire they didn't get the priest's blessing. And Lucile all emotional, as the young mother of the bride. It's just so twisted.

She breaks out laughing, her head thrown back, leaning against the armchair. She laughs, she laughs. Her gaze is fixed, she's completely pale, and thick muscles stand out under the skin of her neck, which has suddenly become the neck of a very old woman. It's the kind of situation where you slap someone or throw water on them, but Laurence doesn't dare. She only says:

— Calm down. Please, please, calm down.

A fire is dying in the fireplace, it's too hot. The laughing stops. Dominique's head returns to its usual position. The neck cords disappear. Her face sags. Say something.

— Has Marie-Claire agreed to a divorce?

— She's only too happy to. She hates me. I bet she'll even be a guest at the wedding. Dominique beats her fist against the side of the armchair.

— I've struggled my whole life. And this stupid little bitch has bagged herself one of the richest men in France at barely twenty years old. She'll still be young when he kicks the bucket and leaves her half his fortune. Do you think that's fair?

— Nothing's fair! Listen: you made it all by yourself, and

that's a beautiful thing. You didn't need anyone else. That proves how strong you are. Show them your strength, that you don't care about Gilbert.

— You think it's a beautiful thing to have to make your own way! You don't know what that means. What you have to go through, and submit to, when you're a woman. My whole life I've been humiliated. With Gilbert . . . her voice fails. With Gilbert I felt protected, at peace, after so many years . . .

The way she says these words makes Laurence feel a rush of love for her. Security; peace. Like a revelation of the truth of her life, which she usually tries so hard to cover up.

— Dominique, darling, you should be proud of yourself. And not feel humiliated ever again. Forget Gilbert, he doesn't deserve your regret. Of course it's hard, it will take some time, but you'll come out on top . . .

— It's not humiliating to be thrown out with the rubbish like an old piece of junk? Oh! I can hear them sniggering.

— There's nothing to snigger at.

— They'll snigger, all the same.

— Then they're idiots. Don't even give them a moment's thought.

— How can I not? You don't understand. You're like your father, you glide along outside everything. But I have to live with these people.

— Don't see them any more.

— Who will I see then? Tears begin to flow on Dominique's

pale face. Being old is bad enough. But I thought Gilbert would be there, that he would always be there. And then: no. Old and alone: it's excruciating.

— You're not old.

— I will be.

— You're not alone. You have me, you have us.

Dominique sobs. Beneath her mask is a flesh-and-blood woman, with a heart, who feels age and solitude upon her, and is terrified. She murmurs:

— A woman without a man is a woman who's alone.

— You'll meet someone else. And until then you have your work.

— My work? You think that means anything to me? At one time, of course, because I was ambitious. Now I've arrived, and I have to ask: where?

— Exactly where you wanted to be. You have an exceptionally good situation; you have a fascinating job.

Dominique isn't listening. Her gaze is fixed on the wall in front of her.

— A woman who's arrived! From the outside it looks impressive. But when you find yourself alone in your room at night . . . you know you'll be alone for ever. She is shaking, as if coming out of a trance. I can't bear it! But we do, we do, says Gilbert. Yes or no?

— Take a trip. Go to Baalbek without him.

— Alone?

— With a friend.

— Do I have any friends? And where would I find the money? I don't know if I can even keep Feuverolles, it's too expensive to maintain.

— Take your car, drive to Italy, it'll be a good change of scene.

— No, no! I won't give in. I've got to do something.

Dominique's face hardens and Laurence feels vaguely fearful.

— What? What will you do?

— Somehow I'll get my revenge.

— How?

Dominique hesitates, and her mouth deforms into something like a smile.

— I'm sure they've kept the little one in the dark about her mother's relationship with Gilbert. I'll tell her about it. And also how he used to talk about her body – her breasts and everything else.

— You can't do that! That would be madness! You can't go and see her.

— No. But I can write to her.

— You can't be serious.

— Why not?

— That would be a revolting thing to do.

— Isn't it revolting what they're doing to me? Elegance, fair play, what a joke! They don't have the right to make me suffer. I won't turn the other cheek.

Laurence has never judged Dominique, or anyone else,

but she shivers. It's so dark inside that heart, full of twisting snakes. She has to prevent this at all costs.

— You won't achieve anything. You'll just lower yourself in their eyes, and the wedding will go ahead anyway.

— I doubt that very much. She thinks for a minute, calculating. Patricia is a fucking idiot. It's just like Lucile to have lovers her little girly girl knows nothing about, her little girly girl is a virgin, she deserves her orange flowers . . .

Laurence is stupefied by her mother's sudden vulgarity. She has never spoken in this voice, used this kind of language. It's someone else who's talking, it's not Dominique.

— Well, that angelic little girl is going to learn the truth. I think it's going to give her quite a shock.

— She hasn't done anything to you, you can't blame her.

— I can blame her. Dominique asks aggressively: Why are you defending her?

— I'm trying to save you from yourself. Listen, you've always said we have to swallow our pride; you were so angry with Jeanne Texcier.

— But I'm not killing myself, I'm getting my own back. What to say, what to argue?

— They will say that you're lying.

— She won't speak to them. She'll hate them too much.

— Suppose she does speak to them. They'll tell everyone you wrote those letters.

— Certainly not, they won't want to air their dirty laundry in public like that.

— They will say you've written vile letters, without saying what was inside them.

— Well, I'll say what was inside them.

— What will people think of you?

— That I refuse to let myself be trampled on. At any rate I'm a jilted woman. An old woman thrown aside for a younger one. I would rather be vile than ridiculous.

— I'm begging you.

— You're so tiresome, says Dominique. Fine, I won't do it. So what? That defeated look comes back on to her face, and she bursts into tears.

— I've never had any luck. Your father was completely inept. Yes, inept. And when I finally meet a real man, he leaves me for some twenty-year-old idiot.

— Do you want me to stay the night?

— No. Give me my pills. I'm going to raise the dosage a bit, and I'll sleep. I'm on the other side of it now.

A glass of water, a green capsule, two little white pills. Dominique swallows them:

— You can go now.

Laurence kisses her mother and closes the door behind her. She drives slowly. Is Dominique going to write that letter? How to keep her from doing it? Should she warn Gilbert? That would be a betrayal. And he can't monitor Patricia's post. Should I take Maman away somewhere, right now, tomorrow? She would refuse to go. What should she do? Merely asking the question flusters her. I've always followed the rules, never decided anything for myself, not my marriage, not my career, not my affair with Lucien, it began and it ended, in spite of myself. Things happen to me, that's all. What should she do? Ask Jean-Charles's advice?

— My God, Dominique was in such a state, she says. Gilbert told her everything.

He puts down his book, after sliding a bookmark between the pages.

— You knew he was going to.

— I'd hoped she would take it better. For a month she's said nothing but bad things about him!

— There are so many issues at play. Money, for one thing – she's going to have to change her lifestyle.

Laurence tenses. Jean-Charles hates sentimentality, but still, the indifference in his voice!

— Dominique doesn't love Gilbert for his money.

— But he has money, and that counts for something. It's true for everyone, if you can believe it, he says in an aggressive voice.

She doesn't answer, and stalks off to her room. He's clearly still upset about the eight hundred thousand francs that the accident cost him. And he thinks it's my fault! She undresses briskly, fury rising. I don't want to be angry, I have to get a good night's sleep. A glass of water, some of her gymnastics exercises, a cold shower. Clearly she can't turn to Jean-Charles for advice; he never wants to get involved in other people's business, never. Only one person can help

Laurence: her father. And yet despite the depth of his under-standing, and his generosity, she doesn't want him to wallow in self-pity over Dominique. For once, making a great excep-tion, she takes a sleeping pill before getting into bed. There have been too many emotions since Sunday, everything's happening all at once.

She holds off from calling her mother, she needs her sleep, until she's about to leave for work.

— How are you? Did you get some rest?

— I did, until around four in the morning.

There's a kind of happy challenge in her voice.

— Only until four a.m.?

— Yes, that's when I woke up. She pauses, and then says, triumphantly:

— I wrote a letter to Patricia.

— No! Oh no! Laurence's heart is pounding violently in her chest. Have you sent it?

— By pneumatic post, at five a.m. It makes me deliriously happy to imagine the look on her face, sweet little thing.

— Dominique! That's completely mad. She cannot read that letter. Ring her right now and tell her not to read it.

— You're mad if you think I'm going to ring her up! At any rate it's too late, she's already read it.

Laurence falls silent. She hangs up and has just enough time to run to the bathroom, where a spasm tears across her stomach and she throws up all the tea she drank this morn-ing. She hasn't vomited out of emotion in years. Her stomach emptied, she continues to heave. She can't picture the scene in her mind, she can't imagine how Patricia, or Lucile, or Gilbert might react. But she's afraid. Panicked. She drinks a glass of water and collapses on to the sofa.

— Are you tired, Maman? asks Catherine.

— A little. It's not serious. Go and do your homework.

— You're tired or you're sad? Is it because of Mammie?

— Why do you ask?

— Before you said that she was better, but you didn't seem to believe it.

Catherine raises an anxious but confident face to her mother. Laurence threads her arm around her waist and pulls her close.

— She's not really ill. It's just that she was supposed to get married to Gilbert, but he doesn't love her any more, he's going to marry someone else. So she's unhappy.

— Oh! Catherine thinks for a moment. What can we do?

— Be very, very nice to her. Nothing else.

— Maman, is Mammie going to get mean?

— What?

— Brigitte says that when people are mean it's because they're unhappy. Except for the Nazis.

— She told you that? Laurence holds Catherine even closer. No. Mammie is not going to get mean. But be careful when you see her, don't let on that you know she's sad.

— I don't want you to be sad either, says Catherine.

— I'm happy because I have such a lovely little girl. Go and do your homework, and promise not to say anything to Louise, she's too little.

— I promise.

She kisses her mother's cheek. Must she grow up to be a woman like me, with stones in her chest and sulphurous clouds in her head?

Let's not think about it any more, I don't want to think about it any more, Laurence tells herself as she sits in her office at Publinf talking to Mona and Lucien about the Floribelle fabric launch. Eleven-thirty. Patricia must have received the pneu at eight.

— Are you listening to what I'm saying? says Lucien.

— Of course I am.

He's rigid with resentment and hostility, she'd rather not see him at all, but Voisin won't let him go. The innocence of cotton lawn, sophisticated innocence, transparence. Limpid and clear like spring water, but also naughty and suggestive. They have to work with these contrasts. The telephone rings and Laurence jumps. Gilbert.

— I advise you to go and see your mother immediately.

A cutting, unkind voice, and he hangs up.

Laurence dials her mother's number. She hates this machine, it brings people so close yet so remote, a Cassandra whose harsh voice abruptly breaks into her days, announcing only drama and disaster. On the other end of the line, the phone rings with no answer; the apartment is probably empty. And yet according to Gilbert, Dominique should be there. Somebody in an empty flat, what did that mean? Some body.

— My mother has had an accident. An attack, I don't know what kind, I have to get over there.

She must look very strange. Neither Lucien nor Mona says a word.

She runs, she takes her car and drives as fast as she can, she leaves it by the side of the road where she's not allowed to park, she climbs the stairs four at a time, no time to wait for the lift, she rings three times then knocks twice. Silence. She pushes the bell and doesn't let up.

— Who is it?

— Laurence.

The door opens. But Dominique turns her back on her; she's wearing her blue dressing gown. She goes to her bedroom, where the curtains are drawn. In the semi-darkness Laurence sees a vase on the floor, scattered tulips, a puddle of water on the carpet. Dominique sinks into a low armchair. Like the other day, her head is thrown back, eyes on the ceiling, sobs swelling up her neck so the cords stand out. The front of her robe is torn, some buttons are missing.

— He slapped me.

Laurence goes to the bathroom, opens the medicine cabinet.

— Have you taken a tranquilliser? No? Then swallow this.

Dominique obeys. And she speaks in a voice that belongs to no one. Gilbert buzzed at ten o'clock, she thought it was the concierge, she opened the door. Patricia had immediately gone crying to Gilbert, and Lucile shouted, he kicked the door closed behind him, he stroked Patricia's hair, so tenderly, and spoke to her in such a calm voice, and in the front hall he had insulted her, slapped her, grabbed her by the collar of her dressing gown and dragged her to the bedroom. Dominique's voice is muffled. She hiccups.

— I just want to die.

What happened, exactly? Laurence feels as though her head is on fire. In the disorder of the unmade bed, the torn robe, the flowers on the floor, she sees Gilbert, with his huge well-manicured hands, and the malice on his face a little too crude. Had he dared? Who would have stopped him? Laurence chokes with horror, the horror which must have passed through Dominique during those moments, of what is happening now. Oh! all the images have shattered, they can never be pieced back together. Laurence wants a tranquilliser too, but no, she needs to remain lucid.

— He's an animal, she says. They're all animals.

— I want to die, murmurs Dominique.

— Come! Let's not sit here in tears, that would only make him too happy, says Laurence. Wash your face, take a shower, get dressed, and let's get out of here.

Gilbert had understood that there was one way to wound Dominique in the marrow of her being: humiliation. Would she ever get over it? It would be so easy if Laurence could take her in her arms, stroke her hair, the way she does with Catherine. What tears her apart is the revulsion she feels, mixed with pity. As if she felt bad for a wounded toad, without being able to touch it. She's horrified by Gilbert, but also by her mother.

— He's probably telling Patricia and Lucile everything right now.

— Of course not. Brutalising a woman is nothing to be proud of.

— He is proud, he's going to brag about it everywhere. I know him.

— But he won't be able to say why. You said it yourself yesterday: he's not going to want to tell the whole world that he slept with his fiancée's mother.

— That little slut! She showed him my letter!

Laurence looks at her mother, stupefied.

— But Dominique, I told you she would!

— I didn't believe it. I thought she would be disgusted and leave him. That's what she should have done, given this thing with her mother: keep quiet and get out. But she wants his money.

For years she's treated people like obstacles to be removed, and she's been very good at it, but she's ended up forgetting that other people have the right to their own existence, which doesn't always align with her plans. Trapped by her own hysteria, her dramatics. Always imitating someone else, without knowing what kind of behaviour to adopt in any given circumstance. And people think she's a strong-minded woman, efficient, her own boss . . .

— Get dressed, Laurence repeats. Put on your dark sunglasses, I'm taking you out for lunch somewhere, outside Paris, where we're certain not to meet anyone.

— I'm not hungry.

— It will do you good to eat.

Dominique goes into the bathroom. The tranquilliser has worked. She does her make-up in silence. Laurence throws out the flowers, wipes up the water, calls her office. She gets her mother into the car, Dominique is quiet. She looks very pale behind the big black sunglasses.

Laurence chooses a restaurant with walls entirely made of glass, high up with a sweeping view of the surrounding neighbourhood. There is a banquette at the back of the room. It's expensive, but not elegant; Dominique's friends would never eat here. They choose a table.

— I have to tell my secretary I'm not coming in today, says Dominique.

She slips off, her shoulders slumped. Laurence goes out to the terrace which overlooks the plains. In the distance she sees Sacré-Coeur, sparkling white, and the slate roofs of Paris gleaming under the deep blue sky. It's one of those days when a hint of spring happiness peeps through the December chill.

Birds sing in the barren trees. Cars speed along the autoroute beneath her, glittering in the sun. Laurence doesn't move; it's as if time itself has stopped. Behind this planned, built-up landscape, with its roads, its estates, its housing developments, its cars all in a hurry, something is visible, the sight of which is so affecting that she forgets her troubles, the unending drama, everything, she has become nothing else but lingering expectation, she has no source, and no end. The birds sing, invisible, heralding rebirth, still in the distance. A line of pink hovers on the horizon and Laurence stands for a long while, paralysed by a mysterious emotion. And then she is once again on the terrace of the restaurant. She is cold, and she returns to the table.

Dominique sits down beside her. Laurence hands her the menu.

— I don't feel like anything.

— Choose something anyway.

— Choose for me.

Dominique's mouth trembles. She seems exhausted. Her voice lowers, humble.

— Laurence, please don't speak to anyone about this. I don't want Marthe to know. Or Jean-Charles. Or your father.

— Of course not.

Laurence's throat is tight. She feels a rush of love for her mother, she wants to help her. But how?

— If you only knew what he said to me! It's horrible. He's a horrible man.

Behind her black glasses, there are tears.

— Don't think about it. Forbid yourself from thinking about it.

— I can't.

— Go on a trip. Take a lover. And forget about it.

Laurence orders an omelette, some sole, some white wine. She knows she is going to have to repeat the same things, over and over, for hours. She is resigned to it. But she is eventually going to have to leave Dominique. And what then?

Dominique makes a kind of weird grimace, snide, maniacal.

— Still, I hope I've at least ruined their wedding night, she says.

— I want to find something really stunning for the Dufrènes, says Jean-Charles.

— You should look in Papa's neighbourhood.

Jean-Charles has a special space in his budget for gifts, tips, nights out, entertaining, and unexpected costs, and he manages it with the same attention to order and balance as the others. When they go shopping this afternoon, the amount they will spend will have been set in advance, give or take a thousand francs. It's delicate work. The gift must be neither stingy nor ostentatious, and it mustn't let on that it's the result of careful calculation. Only, and above all, it must please its recipient. Laurence takes a look at the numbers her husband has jotted down.

— Five thousand francs for Goya, that's not very much.

— She's only been with us three months. We can't give what we would if she had worked here all year.

Laurence keeps her mouth shut. She will take ten thousand francs of her own money. It's useful having a job where you receive bonuses unbeknownst to your partner. It's simpler than having to discuss it. There's no use in bothering Jean-Charles; he's certainly going to be unhappy enough about Catherine's school report. Still, she has to work up the courage to show it to him.

— The girls got their marks yesterday.

She hands him Louise's. First, third, second. Jean-Charles looks it over indifferently.

— Catherine's is not as good.

He takes a look and his face darkens: twelfth in French, ninth in Latin, eighth in mathematics, fifteenth in history, third in English.

— Twelfth in French! She always used to come in first! What's happened to her?

— She doesn't like her teacher.

— And fifteenth in history, ninth in Latin!

The comments don't help matters. *Could do better. Talkative in class. Distracted.* Distracted: does she get that from me?

— Have you been to see her teachers?

— I saw her history teacher; Catherine seems tired, or

dreamy, or on the contrary she gets hyperactive and fools around. Girls that age often go through a rough patch, they told me, it's puberty approaching, we're not supposed to worry.

— It seems like more than a rough patch to me. She doesn't do her homework, and she cries at night.

— She's cried twice.

— That's two times too often. Call her in, I want to speak to her.

— Don't scold her. Her grades aren't *such* a disaster.

— Your standards are so low!

In the children's room, Catherine is helping Louise with her decals. It's touching how sweet she is with her sister, ever since she cried about being jealous of Brigitte. There's no contest, Laurence thinks, Louise is pretty, she's funny and clever, but Catherine is my favourite. Why have her grades suffered so? Laurence has some idea, but she is determined to keep it to herself.

— My darling, Papa would like to see you. He's very worried about your grades.

Catherine follows her silently, head slightly lowered. Jean-Charles regards her severely:

— All right, Catherine: explain to me what's happening to you. Last year you were always in the top three. He waves the report in her face. You're not doing your work.

— But I am.

— Twelfth, fifteenth.

She raises an incredulous face to him.

— What difference does it make?

— Don't be insolent!

Laurence intervenes, in an encouraging voice.

— If you want to become a doctor, you'll have to work very hard!

— Oh, I will, because I'll be interested in it, says Catherine. Right now they never talk about things that are interesting.

— History, literature, you don't find that interesting? says Jean-Charles, indignant.

When he argues he always has to be right rather than try to understand where the other person is coming from. Otherwise he would ask her: what does interest you? Catherine wouldn't be able to answer, but Laurence knows – it's the world around her, the world we try to hide from her, but which she glimpses anyway.

— Is it Brigitte's fault you're talking during class?

— Oh no, Brigitte is an excellent student. Catherine raises her voice. She has bad grades in French because the professor is stupid, but she was first in Latin and third in history.

— Well then, you should follow her example. It pains me to think my daughter has become the class clown.

Tears stream down Catherine's face, and Laurence strokes her hair.

— She'll do better next term. Right now she should

enjoy her holiday, forget about school. Go on, my darling, go and play with Louise.

Catherine leaves the room and Jean-Charles says to her angrily:

— If you're just going to fawn over her while I'm scolding her, there's no reason for me to waste my time getting involved.

— She's very sensitive.

— Too sensitive. What's going on with her? She cries, asks questions that are inappropriate for her age, she doesn't do her schoolwork—

— You said yourself that children that age start asking questions.

— Of course. But it's not normal for her grades to suffer like this. I wonder if it's good for her to have a friend who's older than her, and Jewish into the bargain.

— What?

— Don't mistake me for an anti-Semite. But everyone knows Jewish children are worryingly mature for their age and excessively emotional.

— Nonsense, I don't believe that at all. Brigitte is precocious because without a mother she has to get along by herself, and because she has an older brother she's very close to. I'm sure she's an excellent influence on Catherine. She's maturing, she's beginning to ask questions, she's broadening her mind. You take academic success too seriously.

— I want my daughter to succeed in life. Why don't you take her to see a psychologist?

— Absolutely not! You think a child needs to see a psychologist every time they get a bad grade in school?

— Getting bad grades and crying in her sleep. It sounds like a good idea to me. If we take them to see a doctor when they cough I don't see why we shouldn't take her to see someone who specialises in emotional disturbances.

— I don't like the idea at all.

— It's a textbook scenario. Parents become jealous of the psychologists who take care of their children. But we are intelligent enough to avoid that trap. You're a funny one, you know – you're modern in lots of ways, and in others frankly quite backward.

— Backward or not, I think Catherine is just fine as she is. I don't want her ruined.

— A psychologist won't ruin her. He would just get a sense of what's not running smoothly.

— What's not running smoothly? What does that mean? If you ask me things aren't running smoothly for people you think are completely normal. If Catherine is interested in something other than her schoolwork, it doesn't mean her mind is disturbed.

Laurence speaks with such violence that she surprises herself. Usually she keeps to her own path, without straying an inch, without looking left or right. Each age brings its own tasks; if you get angry have a glass of water and do some exercises. It's worked well for me, perfectly well, but they can't make me bring up Catherine that way. She says forcefully:

— I won't keep Catherine from reading whatever books she pleases or from seeing whatever friends she likes.

— You have to admit that she is unbalanced. For once your father was right: knowledge is a wonderful thing but it is dangerous for children. You have to take certain precautions and sometimes protect them from the wrong influences. There's no point in her learning how unhappy life can be right now. There will be plenty of time later.

— That's what you think! It will never be the right time, it's never the right time, says Laurence. Mona is right, we don't understand anything. Every day we read horrible things in the newspapers, and we carry on as if we hadn't.

— Please, don't give me a guilty conscience like you did in '62, says Jean-Charles sharply.

Laurence feels herself go pale, as if he had slapped her. The day she'd read about the woman who was tortured to death she'd started shaking and she couldn't stop; she was beside herself. Jean-Charles had held her tightly, she had let herself go in his arms and he'd said *It's horrible*, and she'd thought he was equally upset. Because of him she had been able to calm down, she had made a significant effort to chase away this memory, and she had just about managed it. It was because of him, essentially, that she had avoided reading the newspapers. But in fact he hadn't cared at all about what happened to that woman, he just said *It's horrible* to appease her, and here he was throwing the incident in her face with such hostility. What a betrayal! So convinced of always being right, furious if we disturb his image of us, the perfect little girl, the perfect young wife, with no interest in who we really are.

— I don't want Catherine to inherit your good conscience.

Jean-Charles hits the table. He doesn't like being stood up to.

— You're the one who's making her unhinged, with your qualms and oversensitivity.

— Me? Oversensitive?

She is completely astonished. She used to have her sensitivities, yes, but Dominique and Jean-Charles had completely starved them of air. Now Mona criticises her indifference, and Lucien says she doesn't have a heart.

— For instance, the other day with the cyclist . . .

— Get out, says Laurence, or I'm leaving.

— I'll go, I have to call in at Monnod's. But you might think about paying a visit to a psychiatrist yourself, he says, getting up.

She locks herself in her bedroom. There is no question of drinking a glass of water or doing her exercises. This time she gives way to her anger, unleashing a hurricane in her chest, shaking every fibre of her being. It hurts, physically, but she feels alive. She sees herself sitting on the edge of the bed, hearing Jean-Charles's voice. *I don't think it was a very clever thing to do, we only have third-party insurance. Everyone would have testified in your favour.* And in a flash of comprehension she realises he wasn't joking. He was actually reproaching me, he is still reproaching me, for not risking a man's life to save him eight hundred thousand francs. The front door closes, he's gone. Would he have done it? At any rate he's angry with me for not having done it.

She remains sitting for a long time, the blood rushing in her head, an oppressive weight on her neck. She wants to cry. Since when has she been unable to?

A record is playing in the children's room, old English songs. Louise is doing her decals, Catherine is reading *Lettres de mon Moulin*. She looks up:

— Maman, was Papa very angry?

— He doesn't understand why your grades have gone down.

— You're angry too.

— No. But I would like you to make more of an effort.

— Papa is angry so often, these days.

It's true that he's been fighting with Vergne, and then the accident; he had been irritated when the girls wanted him to tell them what happened. Catherine noticed his bad moods, she had vaguely felt Dominique's sadness, Laurence's anxiety. Is that the explanation for her nightmares? She had cried three times.

— He's worried. We have to replace the car, and that's expensive. And he's happy to have changed jobs, but that's presented its own problems.

— It's sad to be an adult, Catherine says, convinced.

— No it isn't, we have things to be very happy about. For instance we're happy to have nice little daughters like you.

— Papa doesn't think I'm very nice.

— Of course he does! If he didn't love you so much, he wouldn't care if you had bad grades.

— Do you promise?

— Of course.

Is Jean-Charles right? Does she get her nervous character from me? It's terrifying to think we can influence our children merely by being who we are. A flaming arrow in the heart. Anxiety, remorse. Everyday moodiness, a stray word here and there, or no words at all, all these things that ought to disappear behind me linger on and become a part of this child, who thinks about everything, and who will remember, just as I remember certain inflections in Dominique's voice. It seems unfair. We can't take responsibility for every last thing we do – or don't do. *What are you doing for them?* These things suddenly begin to matter in a world in which nothing really matters. It's too much.

— Maman, asks Louise, are you going to take us to see the nativity?

— Yes, tomorrow or the day after.

— Can we go to midnight mass? Pierrot and Riquet say it's so beautiful, with all the music and lights.

— We'll see.

It's so easy to pacify children with these stories: Fra

Angelico's paradise, wonderful stories about tomorrow, solidarity, charity, aid for developing countries. I refuse some, I accept others, more or less.

Someone's at the door. An abundance of red roses, with a card from Jean-Charles: *Tenderly yours*. She takes out the pins and unwraps the cellophane, she wants to throw them in the bin. A bouquet is never just a bunch of flowers. It's friendship, hope, gratitude, joy. Red roses: passionate love. Except not. It's not even a sincere expression of regret, she's sure of it, it's just a simple nod to conjugal conventions. *Let's not fight during Christmas*. She places the roses in a crystal vase. They're not an expression of blazing passion, but they're beautiful, and it's not their fault they're the bearers of a dishonest message.

Laurence brushes her lips with the perfumed petals. What do I really think of Jean-Charles, deep down? What does he think of me? It seems as if it doesn't matter at all. At any rate we're bound together for life. Why Jean-Charles and not someone else? That's just how it is. (Another young woman, hundreds of young women are, this very minute, asking themselves: why him and not someone else?) No matter what he says or does, no matter what she says or does, there will be no sanctions. Useless to even get angry. There's no way out.

As soon as she heard the key turning in the lock, she ran to the door, thanked him, they embraced. He was glowing because Monnod has put him in charge of a development of prefabricated houses outside Paris: a reliable project which will pay well. He had a quick lunch (she says she ate with the girls, she couldn't swallow a bite) and they left in a taxi to buy presents. They are walking on the rue du Faubourg Saint-Honoré on this frigid cold afternoon. The windows are all lit up, there are Christmas trees in the streets and in the shops, men and women rush by or linger, packages in their arms and smiles on their lips. They say that people who are alone hate the Christmas holidays. I could be surrounded by people and I'd still hate them. The trees, the packages, the smiles, it all unsettles me.

— I would like to buy you a very nice present, says Jean-Charles.

— Don't go overboard. We have to replace the car . . .

— Let's not talk about that any more. I want to go mad and as of this morning I have the cash to do it.

The windows pass slowly by. Scarves, clips, chain bracelets, jewellery for millionaires – a diamond and ruby choker, a string of black pearls, sapphires, emeralds, gold bracelets and bracelets made of precious stones, more modest concoctions of crystal, jade, diamanté, glass bubbles with shiny ribbons inside them, dancing in the light, shiny gold rattan starburst mirrors, blown glass bottles, thick crystal stem vases meant to hold one single rose, blue and white opaline jars, porcelain bottles, black lacquer bottles, powder compacts, some gold, some inlaid with jewels, perfumes, lotions, atomisers, feather gilets, cashmere jumpers, pale jumpers made of wool and camel hair, frothy cool lingerie, soft duvet-like robes in pastel shades, the luxury of lamé, cloqué, brocade, gaufré, filmy woollens frosted with metallic threads, the muted red in the windows at Hermès, the contrast of leather against fur, each setting off the other, clouds of swansdown, filmy lace. And everyone's eyes shining with covetousness, the men's and women's alike.

My eyes used to shine like that. I loved going into all the boutiques, lingering over the profusion of fabrics, wandering in the silken fields scattered with fantastical flowers; I ran my hands through rivers of soft mohair and angora, the coolness of linen, the grace of lawn, the heady warmth of velvet. It was because she loved this paradise, carpeted with luxurious fabrics, trees heaving with gemstones, that she had been able to talk about it immediately. And now she has fallen victim to the slogans she's created. Occupational hazard: as soon as I'm attracted to a setting or an object I wonder whose motivation I am obeying. She was wise to the ruse – all this mystification, all this refinement was too much, and over time came to irritate her immensely. I will detach myself from everything in the end . . . Still, she came to a stop in front of a suede jacket in an undefinable colour: the colour of mist, the colour of time, of fairy stories.

— How beautiful!

— Buy it. But it's not from me. I want to get you something useless.

— No, I don't want to buy it.

She already felt the impulse to leave; this jacket wouldn't have the same shade or texture once it was separated from the three-quarter-length coat the shade of fallen leaves, the smooth leather overcoats, the brilliantly hued scarves that frame it in the window; that's what we're really after, whenever we covet any of the things displayed in it, it's always the whole display we want.

She points at a camera shop.

— Let's go in there. It would make Catherine so happy.

— Of course we're not going to deprive her of presents, says Jean-Charles, sounding preoccupied. But I'm telling you, we have to do something.

— I promise I'll think about it.

They buy an easy-to-use camera. A green light shows if the light is good; if not, it turns red. Impossible to make a mistake. Catherine will be happy. But I wanted to give her something else – security, happiness, the joy of being alive. That's what I'm really selling when I launch a product. A lie. In the window displays, the objects retain the aura that haloed them when they appeared on glossy paper. But once we hold them in our hands, all we see is a lamp, an umbrella, a camera. Lifeless, cold.

Manon Lescaut is full of people – women, a few men, some couples. Newlyweds. They gaze at each other lovingly while he adjusts a bracelet on his wife's wrist. His eyes shining, Jean-Charles clasps a necklace around Laurence's neck.

— Do you like it?

It is beautiful, glittering but simple, but way too luxurious, much too expensive. It's a compensation, a symbol, a substitute. For what? For something that no longer exists, that perhaps never existed at all: a warm, intimate bond that would make any present useless.

— It suits you so well! says Jean-Charles.

Does he feel the weight of things unsaid between us? Not of silence, but of pointless words? Does he not feel the distance, the absence, beneath the politesse of ritual?

She takes off the necklace in a kind of fervour, as if she were delivering herself from a lie.

— No! I don't want it.

— You just said it was your favourite.

— Yes. She smiled weakly. But it's not reasonable.

— That's for me to decide, he says, irritated. But if you don't like it, let's leave it.

She picks the necklace back up. What's the use in making him angry? May as well get it over with.

— I do, I do, I think it's marvellous. It's just that I thought it was a bit extravagant. But after all, it's up to you.

— It's up to me.

She tilts her head again so he can put it back on her: the perfect image of the couple who still adore one another even after ten years of marriage. It's a way of buying conjugal peace, domestic harmony, understanding, love, as well as pride. She looks at herself in the mirror.

— My darling, you were right to insist. I'm ridiculously happy.

Usually, they spend New Year's Eve at Marthe's. *Housewife's prerogative, I have all the time in the world*, she says smugly. Hubert and Jean-Charles split the costs, though there is often friction between them as Hubert is a cheapskate (it's true he doesn't make a fortune) and Jean-Charles doesn't want to have to pay more than his brother-in-law. The previous year the dinner was pretty pathetic. Tonight it should be all right, Laurence concludes after examining the loaded buffet in the corner of the living room, which Marthe has *Christmasified* with candles, a small Christmas tree, a sprig of mistletoe, some holly, tinsel and coloured lights. Their father brought four bottles of champagne given to him by a friend from Reims, and Dominique an enormous foie gras from Périgord, *so much better than foie gras from Strasbourg, the best foie gras in all of France.* With the boeuf en daube, the rice salad, the nibbles, the fruit, the petit-fours, the bottles of wine and whisky, there's more than enough to eat and drink for ten people.

The other years, Dominique spent the Christmas holidays with Gilbert. It was Laurence's idea to invite her tonight. She asked her father:

— You won't be too put out? She's so alone, so unhappy.

— It's all the same to me.

No one knew the details, but everyone knew about the break-up. The Dufrènes were there, brought by Jean-Charles, and Henri and Thérèse Vuillenot, friends of Hubert's. Dominique was *family party ready*, dressed like a *young grandmother* in a simple honey-coloured jersey dress, her hair more white than blonde. She smiled sweetly, almost timidly, and spoke very slowly; she's taking too many tranquillisers, which make her seem so numb. As soon as she's alone, her face falls. Laurence goes to her:

— How was your week?

— Not too bad; I slept fairly well.

Mechanical smile. It looks as though she's pulling up the corners of her mouth with two little strings. Then she lets them go.

— I've decided to sell the house at Feuverolles. I can't keep a big operation like that going all by myself.

— That's too bad. If only we could figure something out . . .

— What would be the point? Who would I have over now? All the interesting people – Houdan, the Thirions, the Verdelets – Gilbert's the one they came to see.

— They would come to see you!

— Do you believe that? You still don't know much about life. In social terms, a woman is nothing without a man.

— Not you, come on. You have a name. You are someone.

Dominique shakes her head.

— Even with a name, a woman without a man is

basically a failure, a kind of outcast. I see how people look at me now. Believe me, it's nothing at all like before.

This is one of Dominique's obsessions: abandonment.

A record is playing, Thérèse is dancing with Hubert, Marthe with Vuillenot, Jean-Charles with Gisèle, and Dufrène extends a hand to Laurence. They all dance very badly.

— You look magnificent this evening, says Dufrène.

She catches a glimpse of herself in a mirror. She is wearing a black fur and this necklace that she doesn't like. It is pretty, though, and it was also to make her happy that Jean-Charles bought it. She finds herself nondescript. Dufrène has already had a bit to drink, his voice is more urgent than usual. He's a nice man, a good friend for Jean-Charles (even if deep down they don't really like each other, they are jealous of each other, more like), but she doesn't particularly care for him.

Someone changes the record, and they swap partners.

— Dear madam, would you grant me this dance? asks Jean-Charles.

— With pleasure.

— It's funny to see them together again! says Jean-Charles.

Laurence follows his gaze. She sees her father and Dominique sitting across from each other, talking cordially. Yes, it is funny.

— She seems to have come out on top, says Jean-Charles.

— She's stuffing herself with tranquillisers and muscle relaxants.

— You know, they ought to get back together, says Jean-Charles.

— Who?

— Your father and mother.

— Are you mad?

— Why?

— They have completely different tastes. She's a socialite and he's a hermit.

— They're both lonely.

— That has nothing to do with it.

Marthe stops the record.

— Five minutes to midnight!

Hubert grabs a bottle of champagne.

— I know an excellent way to uncork a bottle of champagne. I saw it on TV the other day.

— I saw. I have my own technique, which works better.

— Off you go, then.

Each one pops a cork, without spilling a drop, and they are each extremely proud (although they both would have been happier if the other had failed). They fill the glasses.

— Happy New Year!

— Happy New Year.

They clink their glasses, exchange kisses, and laugh. From outside comes the annual blare of car horns.

— What a horrible noise! says Laurence.

— They've been given five minutes, like children who absolutely have to shout between two classes, says her father. And these are civilised adults.

— Well, we have to celebrate somehow, says Hubert.

They open the two other bottles, and go to get the presents piled up behind the couch, they break the coloured strings, untie the ribbons, unfold the brilliantly coloured wrapping paper, printed with stars and trees, sneak looks at each other out of the corners of their eyes, to see who has won the potlatch. *We have*, thinks Laurence. For Dufrène they have found a watch which indicates the time in France and in all the other time zones; for her father, a beautiful telephone, an imitation of an old-fashioned one, which will look very nice next to his old gas lamps. Their other gifts are less original, but all very refined. Dufrène had opted to give everyone gadgets. He gave Jean-Charles a *vénusik* – an indefatigable heart that beat seventy *glops* per minute – and Laurence an *automogale* which if it does, as promised, replicate the song of a nightingale she will never dare attach it to the wheel of her car as she's meant to do. Jean-Charles is delighted, he adores pointless things that do nothing in particular. She also received gloves, perfumes, handkerchiefs, and was in ecstasies over each gift, exclaiming, thanking.

— Go and get some napkins and cutlery and help yourselves, sit wherever you like, says Marthe.

A hubbub ensues, the clatter of plates, it's delicious, have some more. Laurence hears her father's voice.

— You didn't know that? You have to bring the wine to room temperature after you uncork it, not before.

— It's remarkable.

— Jean-Charles chose it.

— Yes, I know a very good little shop.

Jean-Charles can drink a corked wine and call it excellent but he plays the connoisseur, like everybody else. She downs a glass of champagne. They laugh, they joke, and she doesn't think any of their jokes are funny. Last year . . . Well! She didn't have much fun last year either, but she pretended. This year, she doesn't feel like forcing herself. Over time it becomes just too tedious. And then last year she had Lucien to think of, a means of escape. She thought of him as someone she would have liked to be with; missing him was a little romantic flame that kept her warm. But now there's nothing left to miss. Why did she decide to open up a void in her life? To save some time and energy, to spare her heart, when she doesn't know what to do with her time, her energy, her heart? Is her life too full? Too empty? Too full of empty things? What a mess!

— Still, if you compare the lives of different Capricorns, or different Geminis, within each group there are disconcerting similarities, says Dufrène.

— Come on! The truth is, today we've become such

positivists that people have needed to turn to something higher than themselves. We build electronic machines and we read *Planète*.

Laurence is gladdened by her father's vehemence; he has stayed so young, younger than all of them.

— It's true, says Marthe. I'd rather read the Gospel and believe in the mysteries of religion.

— Even religion is losing its sense of mystery, says Mme Vuillenot. It's absolutely deplorable that they've started performing the mass in French, and playing modern music into the bargain.

— Oh, I don't agree, says Marthe in her exalted voice. The Church must keep up with the times.

— Only to a certain point.

They move off together to continue their conversation, not to be overheard by impious ears.

Gisèle Dufrène asks:

— Did you see the retrospective on television yesterday?

— Yes, says Laurence. It seems we've been through quite a year. I hadn't realised.

— They're all like that, and yet we never notice.

We watch the news, we see the photos in *Match*, and we forget them as time goes on. Seeing them all at once is somewhat astonishing. The bloody corpses of whites, of Blacks, buses at the bottoms of ravines, twenty-five children killed, others cut in two, fires, the twisted carcasses of aeroplanes after a crash, a hundred and ten passengers dead just like that, hurricanes, floods, entire countries devastated, villages in flames, race riots, civil wars, long lines of haggard refugees. It was so dismal it was almost laughable. We watch these catastrophes while comfortably ensconced in our homes, and we can't really say the world intrudes on us – all we see are images, framed by the small television screen, bereft of the weight of their reality.

— I wonder what we'll think, in twenty years, of the film about France in twenty years, says Laurence.

— In some cases we'll laugh at these predictions, says Jean-Charles. But on the whole, it will all come true.

In stark contrast with these scenes of disaster, they've been shown the France of the future. The triumph of urbanism: radiant cities everywhere, a hundred and twenty metres tall, hives of activity dripping with light. Autoroutes, laboratories, universities. The only drawback, explains the journalist, is that the French will stagger under the weight of all this abundance, that they will risk losing their drive and energy. They showed images of nonchalant young people who can barely bother to put one foot in front of the other. Laurence hears her father's voice:

— I think we'll start to see in about five years that on the whole, these planners and associated prophets will have got it completely wrong.

Jean-Charles looks at him with an air of somewhat weary superiority:

— You seem to be unaware that in our time, predicting

the future is becoming an exact science. Have you never heard of the Rand Corporation?

— No.

— It's an extremely wealthy American organisation. They interview specialists in every discipline and then they look at the average responses. They work with thousands of scientists, throughout the world.

Laurence is irritated by his superior air.

— Anyway, when they say that the French will lack for nothing . . . You don't need to consult thousands of scientists to find out that in twenty years most people still won't have toilets because they don't put them in most of the HLMs – only showers.

This little fact had scandalised her when Jean-Charles showed him his plans for prefabricated housing.

— Why aren't there any toilets? asks Thérèse Vuillenot.

— The pipework is very expensive, which raises the cost of the housing, Jean-Charles explains.

— What if the profits were reduced?

— My dear, if they lowered the profits too much, there'd no longer be any incentive left to build, says Vuillenot.

His wife looks at him without affection. Of the four young couples, who is still in love? Why would anyone love Hubert, or Dufrène, why does anyone love anyone else, after the first sexual flames have died down?

Laurence drains two glasses of champagne. Dufrène

explains that in property development, it's hard to tell the difference between speculation and fraud. People break the law left and right.

— But that's very worrying, says Hubert, who seems genuinely upset.

Laurence exchanges an amused smile with her father.

— I can't believe that's true, he says. If it matters to you, there must certainly be a way to stay honest.

— By finding another career.

Marthe changes the record, and they go back to dancing. Laurence tries to teach Hubert the jerk. He throws himself into it, panting, the others look at him mockingly, she abruptly gives up and goes over to her father, who is having a debate with Dufrène.

— *Unfashionable*, that's the only word you can say. The classic novel is unfashionable. Humanism is unfashionable. But when I defend Balzac or humanism, maybe I'm in fashion in the future. Nowadays, you spit on abstraction. So I was ahead of you ten years ago, when I refused to fall for it. No. There are other things, apart from fashion. There are values, there are truths.

She has often thought the very same thing. Well, I haven't thought it in those terms, but now that she hears them she can recognise them as her own. She believes in certain values and truths which are resistant to fashion. But which ones, exactly?

Abstraction no longer sells, but neither does figuration,

there's a crisis in painting, what can you do, it's all been so inflated. Lather, rinse, repeat, and so on and so forth. Laurence is bored. I'd like to propose a test, she thinks. You have third-party insurance, a cyclist throws himself under your wheels, do you kill the cyclist or total the car? Who would honestly choose to pay eight hundred thousand francs to save the life of a man they didn't know? Papa, obviously. Marthe? I have my doubts, and in any case she's but an instrument between the hands of God; if he chose to send her that poor boy . . . What about the others? If they had the reflex to avoid the guy, I'm sure they would regret it later. *Jean-Charles wasn't kidding.* How many times a week has she replayed this phrase in her head? She still is. Am I abnormal? A head case, an anxious-depressive? What is wrong with me that isn't wrong with them? I don't care about the redhead, but it's disgusting to me to think of running him over. It's Papa's influence. For him you can't put a price on a human life, even if he thinks all men are pathetic. And money doesn't mean anything to him. It does to me, but much less than all the rest of them. Her ears perk up because her father is speaking. He's a lot less taciturn tonight than he has been in other years.

— The castration complex! It explains nothing, while pretending to explain everything. I can imagine a psychiatrist coming to see a man on death row the morning of his execution to find him in tears – what a castration complex! he would say.

They laugh, and go back to talking.

— Are you trying to think up an idea? For which new product?

Laurence's father smiles at her.

— No, I was just daydreaming. I get so bored by all their talk of money.

— I understand. They genuinely think money brings happiness.

— You have to admit that it helps.

— I'm not so sure. He sits down beside her. I hardly see you any more.

— I've had to spend a lot of time looking after Dominique.

— She's not as fierce as she once was.

— That's the depression.

— And you?

— Me?

— How are you?

— The holidays have been tiring. Soon it'll be time for the white goods show.

— You know what I was thinking. You and I should go away somewhere together.

— Just us?

An old dream come true: she used to be too young, and then Jean-Charles and the children came along.

— I have some time off in February and I'd like to take advantage of it to revisit Greece. Could you arrange it so you could come with me?

Fireworks of joy. It would be easy to get a couple of

weeks off in February, and I have some money in my account. But do dreams really come true?

— If the children are all right, if everything is in order, I could perhaps arrange it. But it seems too good to be true . . .

— You will try!

— Absolutely. I will try.

Two weeks. I'd finally have time to ask him questions, get answers, to everything I've been wanting to know for years. I would get to know what his tastes are. I would understand the secret of what makes the two of us so different from everyone else, the reason why I love him like no one else.

— I'll do all I can to make it work. But what about you – you won't change your mind?

— Cross my heart and hope to die, he says solemnly, like when she was a little girl.

4

I remember seeing one of Buñuel's films. None of us had liked it, and yet for some time now it has been haunting me. Locked in a magic circle, these people repeat a random moment from their past. They go back in time and are able to avoid the traps they had fallen into, without knowing it. (Though indeed shortly afterwards, they fall back into them.) I also wanted to go backwards, undo the snares, succeed where I had failed. What did I fail to do? I don't even know. I don't have the words to complain or regret. But the lump in my throat prevents me from eating.

Let's start again. I have plenty of time. I've drawn the curtains. Lying down, eyes closed, I can replay the trip picture by picture, word by word.

The explosion of joy when he asked *Do you want to come to Greece with me?* In spite of everything, I hesitated. Jean-Charles pushed me to go. He thought I was depressed. And I had finally relented that Catherine could see a psychologist. He thought if I weren't there, it would help their relationship.

— It's a pity to have to fly to Athens, said Papa. But I love flying on a jet. The plane suddenly pierces the sky, and it's as though the walls of my prison are crumbling, my narrow little life, circumscribed by so many others, of which I know nothing. The housing developments and all the little houses disappear, I'm flying above all the enclosures, relieved of gravity, above my head unfurls endless blue space, beneath my feet are blindingly white landscapes which don't actually exist. I am elsewhere: nowhere and everywhere. And my father began to talk to me about all the places he wanted to show me, and what we would discover together. And I thought *It's you I want to discover*.

Landing. Warm air, odour of petrol blended with the smell of sea and pine. Pure sky, far-off hills, one of which is called Hymettus — bees gathering nectar from a violet earth — and Papa translated the characters written on the pediments of the buildings: entrance, exit, post office. It was pleasant to return to the childhood mystery of language, when I turned to him to make sense of words and things. *Don't look*, he said on the autoroute. (A bit disappointed to find they'd replaced the broken-down old road of his youth.) *Don't look: the beauty of a temple is connected to the site where it is constructed; to appreciate its harmony it must be observed from a certain distance, from a particular perspective. Unlike our cathedrals, which are just as moving — if not more so — from close up as they are from far away*. I found these warnings very sweet. And he was right, perched on its hill the Parthenon looked like those fake alabaster reproductions you can buy in souvenir shops. No charm at all. But it didn't matter to me. What mattered was driving next to Papa in the orange and grey DS – these flamboyantly coloured Greek taxis, blackcurrant sorbet, lemon ice cream – with twenty days ahead of us. I went into the hotel room, I put away my clothes without feeling like I was a tourist in a commercial: everything that was happening to me was real. In the plaza, which felt like an enormous café terrace, Papa ordered me a cherry drink, cool, light, slightly sour, deliciously juvenile. And I understood that word we read in books: happiness. I had known joys, pleasures, pleasure, minor triumph, tenderness; but this conjunction of a blue sky and a fruity drink, of the past and the present brought together in a beloved face, and this feeling of internal peace – this I didn't know, except in very ancient memory. Happiness: life proving its own point. It enveloped me while we ate grilled lamb in a tavern. We could see the wall of the Acropolis bathed in orange light and Papa said it was a sacrilege but I thought everything was beautiful. I liked the medicinal taste of the retsina. *You are the ideal travelling companion*, Papa said, smiling. He smiled again the next day at the Acropolis because I zealously listened to him while he explained about the cyma, the drip-stone, mutule, gutta, abacus, the echinus, and the gorge of the capital; he drew my attention to the slight curve which softened the severity of the horizontal lines, the slight inclination of the vertical columns, their shapes, the subtle refinement of their proportions. It was a little cold, the wind blew under a clear sky. From far off I could see the hills, the sea, the dry little houses the colour of brown bread, and Papa's voice flowed through me. I felt good.

— There are many reasons to criticise the West, he said. We have made very serious mistakes. But all the same, here man has realised himself, and expressed himself in an unequalled manner.

We rented a car, we visited the nearby areas, and every day, before the sun went down, we climbed the Acropolis, the Pnyx, or the Lycabettus. Papa refused to go into the modern city. *There's nothing to see there*, he told me. In the evening he took me to a little local restaurant, on the advice of a friend: in a cave beside the sea, decorated with fishing nets, shells, and hurricane lamps. *It's more fun than those big places your mother likes so much*. For me it was a tourist trap like any other. Instead of elegance and comfort, they were selling local colour and a discreet feeling of superiority over the sheep who flocked to the luxury hotels. (The theme of the ad would have been: be *different*, or *another* kind of place.) Papa exchanged a few words of Greek with the owner and – like all his clients, but it made everyone feel special – he let us go into the kitchen and raise the lids of the pots. They explained the menu with great specificity and care. I ate hungrily and indifferently.

Marthe's voice:

— Laurence! You absolutely must eat something.

— I'm sleeping, leave me alone.

— At least some broth. I'm going to make you some broth.

She interrupted me. Where was I? The road to Delphi. I loved the dry white landscape, the penetrating wind on the summery sea, but all I could see were stones and water, blind to everything my father was pointing out to me. (His eyes, the same colour as Catherine's: seeing different things, but colourful, moving; and me beside them, blind.)

— Look, he was saying. There's the crossroads where Oedipus killed Laius. It was as if it had happened yesterday, and this story directly concerned him. Pythia's lair, the stadium, the temples; he explained every stone to me, I listened, I tried; in vain; the past remained dead. And I was a little tired of being astonished, of exclaiming. The Charioteer of Delphi: *It gives you a kind of shock, no?* I understood what could be seen in that huge green bronze man, but I didn't feel a shock. I felt some discomfort and even some remorse. I preferred the times we spent sitting in a little bistro drinking ouzo. He told me all about his travels long ago, how he would have liked for Dominique to have gone with him, and us as well when we were old enough.

— To think she's seen Bermuda and America but not Greece or Italy! Still, he said, I think she's changed for the better. Maybe because of this blow she's had, I don't know. She's more open, mature, softer – more lucid.

I didn't contradict him; I didn't want to deprive my poor mother of the few scraps of friendship he accorded her.

Is it from Delphi that we should start travelling back in time? We were sitting in a café overlooking the valley; through the bay windows we could see the night was cold and pure, and full of stars. A small band was playing; there were two couples of American tourists, and plenty of local people: lovers, groups of boys, families. A little girl began to dance. She was three or four – tiny, with brown hair and eyes, a little yellow dress down to her knees, white socks; she was spinning around, her arms over her head, her face lost in ecstasy, looking completely mad. Transported by the music, enchanted, intoxicated, transfigured, wild. Her calm, heavy-set mother was engrossed in conversation with another large woman, while pushing a pram back and forth. Unmoved by the music, by the night, she cast from time to time a bovine gaze at her little visionary.

— Do you see that little girl?

— Charming, Papa said indifferently.

A charming little girl who would grow up to be that matron. No. I didn't want that. Had I drunk too much ouzo? I was possessed by this child who was possessed by the music. That impassioned moment had no ending. The little dancer would never grow up, for eternity she would turn and turn and I would watch her. I refused to forget, to become once again a young woman travelling with her father; I could not allow her to grow up to be like her mother, no longer even remembering that she had once been this adorable maenad. Condemned to death, an atrocious death without a body. Life would assassinate her. I thought of Catherine, whom we were currently assassinating.

I said abruptly:

— I should never have agreed to let Catherine see a psychologist.

Papa looked at me, surprised. Catherine was no doubt very far from his thoughts.

— What made you think of that?

— I think of it often. I am preoccupied. My hand was forced, and I regret my decision.

— I can't imagine it could do any harm, Papa said vaguely.

— Would you have sent me to a psychologist?

— Oh, no.

— You see?

— Well, I don't know, the question never arose. You were so even-tempered.

— I was very upset in '45.

— You had good reason to be.

— And today there isn't a good reason?

— Yes, there is indeed. No doubt it's always normal to be frightened when we begin to discover the world.

— So if we reassure her, we make her abnormal, I said.

It was glaringly obvious, and it was devastating. Under the pretext of curing Catherine of her *sensitivities*, which Jean-Charles was so concerned about, we would be mutilating her. I felt the urge to go home the very next day, to take her back from them.

— In my case, I prefer it when people manage things on their own. Deep down, I think – don't tell anyone, they'll call me a backwards old man – that all this psychology is mere quackery. You will find Catherine just as you left her.

— You think so?

— I'm convinced of it.

He started talking about the outing he had planned for the next day. He wasn't taking my concerns seriously, which was natural enough. Whereas I wasn't as interested in the ancient stones which so fascinated him. It would have been unfair of me to resent him for it. No, it wasn't at Delphi that the line broke.

Mycenae. Maybe it was at Mycenae. When was the moment, exactly? We climbed up a gravel path; the wind was lifting up whirlwinds of dust. Suddenly I saw this doorway, with its two decapitated lions, and I felt – was it the shock my father had told me about? I would say rather – a panic. I followed the Royal Road, I saw the terraces, the murals, and the very countryside which Clytemnestra saw when she scanned the horizon for Agamemnon's return. It felt like being torn from myself. Where was I? I didn't belong to the century when people came and went, slept and ate in this still undamaged palace. And my own life had nothing to do with these ruins. What is a ruin, anyway? It's neither the present nor the past; and it's not eternity either; one day it will disappear, no doubt. I said to myself *It's so beautiful!* and I nearly staggered, swept up in a whirlwind, tossed about, negated, reduced to nothingness. I would have liked to go running back to the tourist office and spend the whole day reading mystery novels. A group of Americans were taking photographs.

— What barbarians! said Papa. They take pictures so they don't have to look at where they are.

He told me about Mycenaean civilisation, the grandeur of the Atreides, of their downfall, which Cassandra foresaw; guidebook in hand, he tried to identify every inch of the site. And I thought that he was basically doing the same thing as the tourists he had mocked – trying to open his life to the traces of a time that was not his own. They would glue their photographs into an album, and show them to friends. He would carry these images in his mind, along with their captions, and file them away in the museum of his mind. I had neither an album nor a museum; I received this beauty, and could find nothing to do with it.

On the way back I said to Papa:

— I envy you.

— Why?

— These things mean so much to you.

— And not to you?

He seemed disappointed, so I said brightly:

— They do! But I don't understand them as well. I don't have your education.

— Then read the book I gave you.

— I will read it.

But even if I read it, I thought, it won't bowl me over to think that they've found the name Atreus on tablets in Cappadocia. I could not suddenly will myself to become wildly enthusiastic about stories of which I knew nothing. It would have taken many years of living with Homer and the Greek tragedies, to have travelled a great deal, to know how to compare things. All these dead centuries seemed so foreign to me, they crushed me completely.

A woman dressed in black emerged from a garden and motioned to me. I went to her, and she held out a hand, babbling something. I gave her a few drachmas. I said to Papa:

— Did you see?

— Who? The beggar woman?

— She wasn't a beggar. She was a peasant, and not even very old. It's terrible, a country where peasants have to beg.

— Yes, Greece is a poor country, said Papa.

When we stopped off in some small village, I was often disturbed by the contrast between such beauty and such misery. Papa had assured me, one day, that the really poor communities – in Sardinia, in Greece – manage to attain an austere contentment, thanks to their ignorance of money and various values which we ourselves have lost. But the Peloponnese villagers didn't seem happy at all, not the women breaking rocks by the side of the road, nor the little girls carrying pails of water that were far too heavy for them. I turned away. We were not there to take pity on them. But still, I wished that Papa would tell me where he had met these people who were contented by their deprivation.

At Tiryns, at Epidaurus, I found here and there the feelings I'd experienced in Mycenae. I was very happy the evening of our arrival at Andritsaina. It was late, we had driven by moonlight on a bumpy road beside a cliff; Papa seemed engrossed by his task as he drove. We were both a little sleepy and we felt as though we were alone in the world, sheltered in our moving house by the soft glow of the dashboard, our headlights creating a path in the darkness.

— There is a charming hotel, said Papa. Rustic and well looked-after.

It was eleven o'clock when we pulled into the small central square of the village, beside an inn with closed shutters.

— That's not Mr Kristopoulos's inn, he said.

— Let's go and find it.

We wandered on foot through the tiny, deserted streets. Not a window was lit; there was no other hotel besides this one. Papa knocked at the door: no answer. It was very cold outside; sleeping in the car would not have been much fun. We shouted and knocked again. From the other side of the street a man came running. Inky black hair and moustache, dazzling white shirt.

— You're French?

— Yes.

— I heard you calling out in French. It's market day tomorrow, the hotel is full.

— You speak French very well.

— Oh, not well. But I love France.

When he smiled it was as bright as his shirt. Mr Kristo-poulos's hotel no longer existed, but he would find us some beds. We followed him; I was charmed by the adventure. It was the kind of thing that would never happen with Jean-Charles: we leave, we arrive on time and in any case he's always reserved rooms in advance.

The Greek man knocked at a door, and a woman appeared at the window. Yes, she would rent us two rooms. We thanked our guide.

— I would so like to meet you for a while tomorrow morning, to talk about your country, he said.

— With pleasure. Where?

— There is a café in the square.

— All right. Does nine o'clock suit?

— Yes.

In a room with a red tiled floor, under piles of blankets, I slept like a log until Papa's hand on my shoulder woke me in the morning.

— We came on the right day – the market is on. I don't know if you're anything like me but I love markets.

— I would love to see this one.

The square was full of women in black sitting in front of baskets placed on the ground: eggs, goat's cheese, cabbage, a few skinny chickens. Our friend waited for us in front of the café. It was cold, the market women must have been freezing.

We went inside. I was dying of hunger, but there was nothing to eat. The scent of the dark, thick coffee consoled me.

The Greek man began to speak to us in French. He was so happy whenever he met French people! How lucky we were to live in a free country! He so loved to read French books, French newspapers. He lowered his voice, no doubt more out of habit than prudence:

— In your country you don't put people in prison for their political opinions.

Papa had an air of understanding which astonished me. He knows so many things, but he's so modest you don't realise it. He asked, his voice quiet:

— Is the repression still quite severe?

The Greek man nodded.

— The Aegina prison is full of communists. And if you knew how they were treated!

— Is it just as bad as in the camps?

— Just as bad. But they won't break us, he added emphatically.

He interrogated us on life in France. Papa gave me a conspiratorial glance and began to speak of the difficulties for the working class, its hopes, its achievements; you would have thought he was a card-carrying member of the Party. I was having fun but my stomach was cramping. I said:

— I'm going to see if I can find something to buy.

I wandered through the square. Women who were also dressed in black were chatting with the market women. *An austere contentment*: that's not what I read on their faces, red with cold. How could Papa have been so wrong about that, when he is usually so perceptive? No doubt he had only visited these places in summer: with the sun, the fruit and the flowers, they are surely more joyful then.

I bought two eggs that the stallholder soft-boiled for me. I took the top off one and there was a terrible smell; I opened the other and it was rotten too.

— How is that possible? They arrive straight from the farm.

— The market takes place every two weeks. If we're lucky we get the eggs from the day before. But otherwise . . . It's better to eat the eggs hard-boiled, I should have warned you.

— I would rather not eat them at all.

A little later, on the road to the temple of Bassae, I said to Papa:

— I didn't know that Greece was so impoverished.

— The war ruined it, especially the civil war.

— He was nice, that man. And you played your part to perfection. He was convinced that we were communists.

— I have a lot of respect for the communists here, because they risk going to prison, or even losing their lives.

— Did you know there were so many political prisoners in Greece?

— Of course. I have a colleague who bombarded us with petitions to sign against the Greek camps.

— Did you sign?

— Once I did, yes. In general I refrain from signing anything. First of all because it's perfectly useless. And then because behind these initiatives which seem so humanitarian, there is always political manoeuvring.

We returned to Athens and I insisted we go to see the modern city. We walked around Omonia Square. Doleful-looking people, badly dressed, the smell of grease.

— You see, there's nothing to see, said Papa.

I would have liked to find out what was happening behind these extinguished faces. In Paris, too, I know nothing of all the people I brush past in the street, but I am too busy to care; whereas in Athens I had nothing else to do.

— We should meet some Greek people, I said.

— I've known some. They weren't very interesting. And in any case, these days, people are all the same, regardless of their country.

— Still, the problems they have here are not the same as in France.

— They are terribly banal, here as there.

The contrast was much more striking than in Paris – for me anyway – between the luxury of the wealthy neighbourhoods and the despair of the crowd.

— I suppose Greece is happier in summer.

— Greece isn't happy, said Papa with the slightest hint of a reproach, it is beautiful.

The Kouroi were beautiful, their lips drawn back into a

smile, their eyes staring ahead; they seemed cheerful and a little stupid. I loved them. I knew I would not forget them and I wanted to leave the museum immediately after having seen them. The other sculptures, the fragments of bas-reliefs, the friezes, the gravestones – I couldn't manage to get interested in them. A great weariness came over me, in body and spirit. I admired Papa, the power of his attention and his curiosity. In two days I would leave him knowing no more about him than when we arrived. This thought that I had been holding back for – how long? suddenly went through me. We walked into a room filled with vases, and I could see ahead of us room after room, all full of vases. Papa stopped in front of a display case and began to reel off periods and styles and all their characteristics: Homeric period, Archaic period, black-figured vases, red-figured vases, white-ground vases; he explained what the scenes on their sides were depicting. Though he stood right beside me he got further and further away, all the way to the end of the suite of rooms with their shiny parquet floors. Or it was me who sank like a stone in the abyss of indifference; either way, there was an uncrossable distance between us, because for him, the difference of colour, or a drawing of a palm or a bird, astonished him, pleased him, reminded him of long-ago pleasures, of his whole history. Whereas the vases bored me, and as we went from vase to vase I became exasperated to the point of acute distress, and at the same time I thought: *I've failed at everything*. I stopped short, saying:

— I can't go on!

— Oh dear, you're right, you can hardly stand. You should have said something before!

He was very sorry, supposing no doubt some feminine fragility which brought me suddenly to the point of passing out. He took me back to the hotel. I drank a sherry and tried to talk to him about the Kouroi. But he seemed unreachable, and disappointed.

The next morning I let him go off by himself to the Acropolis museum.

— I'd rather go back to the Parthenon.

The air was gentle; I looked at the sky, the temple, and felt a bitter sense of defeat. Tourist groups and couples listened to the guides with a polite interest, or tried to stifle their yawns. Clever advertising had made them believe that here, they would reach undreamed-of ecstasies, and back home no one would ever admit they hadn't been moved; they would tell all their friends to go and visit Athens, and the chain of lies would perpetuate itself, the pretty pictures would remain undisturbed, untouched by disillusion. Still, I saw a young couple and a pair of slightly older women climb slowly towards the temple, talking to each other, and smiling, and stopping and looking with an air of calm contentment. Why not me? Why am I incapable of loving things that I know are worthy of it?

Marthe comes into the room.

— I made you some broth.

— I don't want any.

— Force yourself to have a little bit.

To make her happy, Laurence swallows a bit. She hasn't eaten for two days. So what? She isn't hungry. Their worried looks. She empties the mug, her heart begins to pound, she's covered in sweat. Just enough time to make it to the bathroom before she vomits, like yesterday and the day before that. What a relief! She would like to completely empty herself, still more, vomit out her entire self. She rinses her mouth, falls back on her bed exhausted, calmed.

— You couldn't keep it down?

— I told you I can't eat anything.

— You absolutely must see a doctor.

— I don't want to.

What could a doctor do? What was the use? Now that she's vomited, she feels good. It is night-time inside her; she has abandoned herself to the night. She thinks of a story she read: a mole feels its way through some underground tunnels, it emerges and feels the cool air, but it cannot discover how to open its eyes. She tells herself the story a different way: the mole in its underground tunnel discovers how to open its eyes, and it sees that everything is dark. Nothing makes any sense.

Jean-Charles sits on the side of her bed and takes her hand.

— My darling, please tell me what's wrong? I just spoke

with Dr Lebel who thinks something has made you very unhappy . . .

— I'm quite well.

— He said it could be anorexia. He's going to drop in later.

— No!

— So then get yourself out of this. Think about it. Anorexia doesn't come about for no reason: find the reason.

She takes back her hand.

— I'm tired, leave me alone.

Something has made her unhappy, yes, she says when he's gone out of the room, but not something so serious as to keep her from getting out of bed or eating. I had a heavy heart in the plane that brought me back to Paris. I hadn't managed to escape my prison, I saw it closing around me when the plane plunged through the fog.

Jean-Charles was waiting at the airport.

— Did you have a good trip?

— Wonderful!

She wasn't lying, she wasn't telling the truth. All the words we say! Words . . . At home, the girls greeted me with cries of joy, jumping all over me, kissing me and asking all kinds of questions. There were flowers in all the vases. I gave them dolls, skirts, shawls, albums and photos and I began to tell them about my wonderful trip. And then I put my clothes away in my wardrobe. I didn't feel as though I was playing the role of a young mother returning home: it was worse. I wasn't a picture, but I wasn't anything else, either. I was nothing. The stones of the Acropolis were no more foreign to me than this apartment. Except for Catherine . . .

— How is she?

— Very well I think, said Jean-Charles. The psychologist wants you to ring her as soon as you can.

— All right.

I chatted with Catherine; Brigitte had invited her to spend the Easter holidays with her, in a house her family had by the Lac des Settons, was that all right? Yes. She knew very well that I would say yes, and she was happy. She got on very well with Mme Frossard; at her house she drew, she played with toys, she had fun.

It's a classic rivalry, perhaps, that arises between mother and psychiatrist; in any case, I couldn't avoid it. I had met Mme Frossard twice, and hadn't particularly liked her either time. She seemed friendly enough, and competent; she asked the right questions, and quickly processed and noted down the answers. When I left her the second time, she knew almost as much about my daughter as I do. Before I left for Greece, I telephoned her. She didn't have anything to tell me; the treatment had barely begun. *And now?* I wondered, as I rang the bell. I was on the defensive, barbed wire all over. She didn't seem to notice, and explained the situation in a cheerful voice. Overall, Catherine is emotionally well-balanced; she loves me very much, and her little sister as well; not quite enough where her father is concerned, he needs to make more of an effort. Her feelings for Brigitte are completely normal, nothing excessive. It was only that she was older and more precocious than Catherine, and their conversations seem to upset her.

— However she promised to be careful, and she does keep her word.

— But how can you expect a twelve-year-old girl to watch what she says? Perhaps she keeps some things to herself, but others seem to have a negative effect on Catherine. In her drawings, her free association, her responses to tests, her anxiety is obvious.

Deep down I knew. I didn't need Mme Frossard to tell me that I had asked the impossible of Brigitte: friendship involves speaking with an open heart. The only way to protect Catherine from the things she said would be to keep the two girls from seeing one another: that was what Mme Frossard was implying. It wasn't a case of a passionate childhood attachment which it can be dangerous to try to nip in the bud. But if we tried to tactfully put a bit more time in between their play dates, Catherine would not be as affected. I had to make sure that between now and the summer holidays, they would see less of each other, and to see to it that the following year they were placed in different classes. It would also be good to find other, less mature friends for my daughter.

— You see! I was right, said Jean-Charles, triumphant. It's that little girl who destabilised Catherine.

I can still hear her voice, I can see Brigitte again, the safety-pin fixing her buttonhole. *Bonjour, m'dame.* The knot returns to my throat. A friendship is a precious thing. If I had a friend, I would talk to her, instead of being so listless.

— First things first, we'll keep her home over Easter.

— She won't like that.

— She will if we offer her something more enticing.

Jean-Charles perked up. Catherine was fascinated by the photographs I brought back from Greece – maybe we should take the girls to Rome! And when we get back we can find things to keep her busy – sports, or dance classes. Horse-riding! What a brilliant idea, even on an emotional level. Replace her friend with a horse?! I tried to dissuade him, but Jean-Charles had made up his mind. Rome and riding lessons.

Catherine seemed bewildered when I told her about the trip to Rome.

— But I promised Brigitte, she will be so disappointed.

— She'll understand. You don't get to go to Rome every day! Don't you want to go?

She is heavy-hearted. But once she gets to Rome she'll be excited to be there, I'm sure of it. She'll hardly think of her friend. With a little manoeuvring she'll have entirely forgotten her by next year.

Laurence's throat tightens. Jean-Charles should not have spoken publicly about Catherine's issues the next day. It was a betrayal, a violation. Romantic exaggeration! But she felt stifled by a kind of shame, as if she were Catherine and had overheard them talking about her. Papa, Marthe, Hubert, Jean-Charles and Laurence had all had dinner at Dominique's house. (Maman getting interested in family reunions! Now I've seen it all! And how chivalrous Papa was towards her!)

— My sister told me about a very similar situation, he said. In year four one of her best friends struck up a friendship with an older girl, whose mother was from Mauritius. Her whole world view changed, and her personality, too.

— Were they kept apart? I asked.

— That I don't know.

— If you consult a specialist, it seems to me that you ought to follow their advice, said Dominique. Don't you think? she said to Papa with a deferential air, as if she thought his opinion of the utmost importance.

She was clearly touched by his solicitude; she had so much need of respect and friendship. What put me ill at ease was that he let himself be taken in by her flirtatiousness.

— It seems logical.

That hesitating voice. And yet at Delphi, when we were watching that little girl dancing madly to the music, he agreed with me.

— If you ask me, the problem lies elsewhere, said Marthe.

She reiterated that for a child, a world without God was unlivable. We don't have the right to deprive Catherine of the consolations of religion.

Hubert ate in silence. No doubt he was working out some torturous exchange of keyrings, his current obsession.

— But it's very important to have a friend! I said.

— You got along very well without them, Dominique replied.

— Not as well as you think.

— Well then, we'll find her another one, said Jean-Charles. This one clearly won't do, since she cries, has nightmares, has let her grades slip, and Mme Frossard finds her slightly unbalanced.

— We have to help her get her equilibrium back. But not by separating her from Brigitte. Papa, when we were at Delphi you said that it was normal to get a bit shaken up as you start to discover the world.

— Some things are normal but still must be avoided; it's normal to yell if you get burned! So you're better off avoiding getting burned. If the psychologist finds her unbalanced . . .

— But you don't believe in psychologists!

I knew I was raising my voice. Jean-Charles gave me a meaningful look.

— Listen, if Catherine has agreed to go away with us without making an issue of it, let's not make one either.

— She's not making it an issue?

— Absolutely not.

— Well then!

Her father and Dominique had said it at the same time:

Well then! Hubert nodded, knowingly. Laurence forced herself to eat, but that's when she had the first spasm. She knew she'd lost. You can't fight off everyone, she's never been arrogant enough to think that. (There had been Galileo, Pasteur, and others that Mlle Houchet recited for us. But I'm no Galileo.) So at Easter – she'll be cured, of course, it's just a matter of a few days, we can go off our food for a few days and it always subsides in the end – they'll take Catherine to Rome. Laurence's stomach contracts. Maybe she won't be able to eat for a while yet. The psychologist would say that she's making herself ill on purpose because she doesn't want to take Catherine away. Ridiculous. If she really didn't want to, she would refuse, she would fight. In the end they would all have to give in.

All of them. Because they're all against her. And once again the image she had repressed so violently was rising with equal violence to the surface, as soon as she let her guard down: Jean-Charles, Papa, Dominique, smiling as if they were on an American advertisement for a brand of oatmeal. And the differences which had seemed so crucial were not so important after all. She alone is different, rejected, unable to live, incapable of loving. She gripped her sheet with both hands. Here it comes, something she fears more than death, one of those moments when everything is collapsing, her body is stone, she wants to scream but stones have no voices, and no tears either.

I hadn't wanted to believe Dominique. Three days after

dinner, eight days after our return from Greece, she said to me:

— Can you imagine? Your father and I are thinking of moving back in together.

— What? You and Papa?

— Is it so astonishing? Why should it be? We have so much in common, after all. A whole history together, and of course you and Marthe and the children.

— Your tastes are so different.

— They were. We've changed a bit as we've got older.

Stay calm, I told myself. There were spring flowers in the living room: hyacinths, primroses. Gifts from Papa? Or had she changed her style? Who was she imitating? The woman she wanted to be? She talked. I let her words wash over me, holding myself back from believing in them, she was so prone to lying to herself. She needed security, affection, esteem. And he felt those things for her, a great deal. He realised that he had misjudged her, that her social life and her ambition were a form of vitality. And he needed someone lively by his side. He felt so lonely, and bored; books, music, culture are all very well but they aren't fulfilling. You had to admit he was still very attractive. And he had evolved. He understood the sterility of his negative attitude. Given his knowledge of parliamentary life she had proposed that he take part in a debate on the radio.

— You can't imagine how happy it made him.

Her voice flowed evenly, contentedly in the warmth of the living room which had once echoed with her terrible sobs. *We bear up though, don't we.* Gilbert was right. We cry, we sob, we wring our hands as if there were something noble about this crying and sobbing and hand-wringing. And it's not even true. Nothing is irreparable because nothing matters. Why not just stay in bed the rest of our lives?

— But hang on, I said. You thought Papa's life was so drab!

I didn't understand. Dominique hadn't suddenly changed her opinion of Papa, she hadn't converted to his world view, or resigned herself to sharing what she called his mediocrity.

— Oh! she said gaily, I'll keep my own. There we are completely in agreement: we'll each have our own occupations and our own friends.

— A kind of peaceful coexistence?

— If you like.

— So why can't you simply be happy to see one another from time to time?

— It's obvious you understand nothing about life, you don't understand at all! said Dominique.

For a moment she was quiet. It was clear that whatever she had cooked up in her mind had nothing disagreeable about it at all.

— I've already told you, a woman without a man is *déclassée* – she's come down in the world. She has no place. I already know that people are whispering about me having gigolos, and there are indeed some who've put themselves forward.

— But why Papa? You could have chosen a more brilliant man, I said, emphasising *brilliant*.

— Brilliant? Compared to Gilbert no one is brilliant. It would look as though I was contenting myself with an imitation. Your father is completely different. A dreamy look came over her face, which matched the hyacinths, the primroses:

— Two married people coming back together after a long separation to face old age side by side: people will be surprised, but they won't snigger.

I was less sure about that than she was, but now I understood. Security, responsibility – these were her primary needs. New affairs would reduce her to the level of a loose woman – and husbands were not that easy to find. I had a glimpse of the person she was trying to become: a woman who's arrived, a woman who's succeeded but has also let go of frivolity in favour of more secret joys, more difficult, more intimate.

But had Papa agreed to all this? Laurence went to see her father that very night. This bachelor's apartment which so pleased her, with its jumble of newspapers and books, its old-fashioned smell. Almost immediately she asked him, forcing herself to smile:

— Is it true what Dominique is saying, that you're going to move back in together?

— Well! though it may surprise you, yes.

He seemed slightly embarrassed, remembering the things he had said about Dominique.

— Yes, I will admit it does surprise me. You seemed so attached to your solitude.

— Moving in with your mother doesn't mean it will go away completely. Her apartment is very big. Naturally, at our age, we both need our independence.

She said slowly:

— I suppose it's a good idea.

— I think so. My way of life is too closed in on itself. One must somehow stay in touch with the world. And Dominique has grown, you know; she understands me much better than she used to.

He talked about one thing and another, and brought up memories of Greece. That very evening she threw up her dinner; she didn't get out of bed the next day, or the day after that, laid out by a thundering succession of images and words running through her head, fighting between them like Malaysian daggers in a closed drawer (if you open it, everything is in order). She opens the drawer. Very simply, I'm jealous. An unresolved Oedipal complex, my mother is still my rival. Electra, Agamemnon. Is that why I was so moved at Mycenae? No. Nonsense. Mycenae was beautiful, I was touched by its beauty. The drawer is closed, the daggers are fighting. I am jealous, but especially, especially . . . She's breathing too quickly, she's panting. It wasn't true, then, that he possessed wisdom and joy and that his own radiance was enough for him! Whatever his secret was, that she had blamed herself for not being able to discover – maybe it didn't exist after all. It didn't exist: she'd known since Greece. I have been *deceived*. The word stabs her. She crushes a handkerchief to her teeth as if to stop the cry she's incapable of holding back. I have been deceived. And I'm right to feel that way. *You can't imagine how happy it made him!* And he'd said: *She understands me better than she used to.* He'd been so flattered. *Flattered*, he who watched the world from on high, with a detached smile, who knew the vanity of all things and who had found serenity beyond despair. He who would never compromise, he went on that radio show, which he accused of lying and servility. He did not belong to some other species. As Mona would say: *Well, what do you know, they're as alike as two peas in a pod.*

She dozed off, exhausted. When she opens her eyes, Jean-Charles is there:

— My darling, you absolutely must allow the doctor to come.

— To do what?

— To talk with you, to try to understand what's happening to you.

She sits up with a start.

— No, never! I won't let you manipulate me. She's shouting. No! No!

— Calm down.

She falls back against her pillow. They'll force her to eat, they'll make her swallow it all down, all what? All that she'll vomit back up, her life, everyone else's with their false loves, their chasing after money, their lies. They will cure her of her refusal, of her despair. No. Why not? The little mole who opens its eyes and sees that it's dark, how will that help him? And Catherine? Are they going to nail her eyelids shut? *No*, she yelled, as loudly as she could. Not Catherine. I won't let them do to her what they've done to me. What have they done to me? This woman who loves no one, insensitive to the beauty of the world, incapable even of crying, this woman I vomit back out. Catherine: on the contrary, open her eyes right away, and maybe a ray of light will filter towards her, maybe she'll be able to get out . . . of what? Of this night. Of ignorance, of indifference. Catherine . . . she suddenly sits back up.

— They won't do to her what they did to me.

— Calm down.

Jean-Charles takes her by the wrist, his gaze wavers as if he wants to call for help; so authoritative, so sure of being right, and the slightest change of plan is enough to scare him.

— I won't calm down. I don't want a doctor. You're the ones who are making me sick, and I will get better all by myself because I won't give in to you. I won't give in where

Catherine is concerned. It's too late for me, I don't care about myself, I've been had, I can't be changed. But her – I won't let them mutilate her. I don't want them to take her friend away, I want her to spend her holidays with Brigitte. And she's not going back to that psychologist.

Laurence throws off the blankets, she gets up, she slips on a robe, she catches Jean-Charles's stunned expression.

— Don't call the doctor, I'm not malfunctioning. I'm just saying what I think, that's all. Oh, don't look at me like that!

— I don't understand any of what you're saying.

Laurence tries to make her voice sound reasonable.

— It's very simple. I'm going to look after Catherine. You get involved from time to time. But I'm the one who's bringing her up, so I'm the one who will make the decisions. I'm making them. Bringing up a child does not mean turning them into a pretty picture . . .

In spite of herself, Laurence's voice is getting louder, she's talking, and talking, and she doesn't know exactly what she's saying, but it doesn't matter, what matters is to shout louder than Jean-Charles and all the others, to reduce them to silence. Her heart is beating very quickly, her eyes are burning:

— I have made my decisions and I won't give way.

Jean-Charles is more and more disconcerted. He murmurs, in a pacifying tone:

— Why didn't you tell me all of this before? There's no use making yourself ill over it. I didn't know you would take all of this so much to heart.

— To heart, yes; maybe I no longer have one, but I certainly take all of this to heart.

She looks him right in the eyes. He turns away, saying:

— You should have mentioned this earlier.

— Maybe you're right. In any case it's done now.

Jean-Charles is stubborn, but deep down he doesn't really take this friendship between Catherine and Brigitte seriously; all of this is far too infantile to really interest him. And it wasn't easy on him, five years ago; he doesn't want me to crack up all over again. If I can keep it together, I will win.

— If you want war, it will be war.

He shrugs:

— A war between us? Who do you think you're talking to?

— I don't know. That depends on you.

— I've never gone against your wishes, says Jean-Charles. He thinks about it. It's true that you look after Catherine much more than I do. When it comes down to it, it's up to you to decide. I've never pretended otherwise. He adds, grumpily, It would have been much simpler if you'd just explained all of this to me from the outset.

She sighs.

— I was wrong. I don't like to go against your wishes either.

They fall silent.

— So we have an agreement? Catherine will spend the holidays with Brigitte?

— If that's what you want.

— It is.

Laurence brushes her hair, touches up her face. For me the die is cast, she thinks, looking at her image in the mirror. She looks pale, drawn. But the girls will have a chance. A chance to do what?

She doesn't even know.

Notes

1. As Elizabeth Fallaize explains in *The Novels of Simone de Beau-voir* (1988), the 'Ferryman's Challenge' is 'a fairly low-grade psychological test, which poses the problem of a woman who, neglected by a husband preoccupied by his work, spends the night with another man at his house on the other side of the river. To get back home early next morning before her husband returns from a trip, she has to recross the bridge, but a madman bars her way. She finds a ferryman but he refuses to work without being paid in advance. Her lover refuses to lend her the money, as does a bachelor friend who lives on the same side of the river; he has always idealised her and declares himself disappointed by her behaviour. After again pleading in vain with the ferryman, she decides to cross the bridge. The madman kills her. The test consists of classing the six characters of the story (in order of their appearance: the woman, the husband, the lover, the madman, the ferry-man, the friend) in order of decreasing responsibility for the woman's death.'